"We have sent Coyote Jones out to Freeway to find Drussa Silver, charge her with violating Galactic Regulation Seventeen, and bring her back here for trial. At the request of the government of Freeway, I might add, which claims that this female charlatan is wreaking havoc with her mumbo-jumbo."

"What mumbo-jumbo?"

"She is," said The Fish patiently, "possessed of unusual psibilities, we are told, and is able to produce mass hallucinations of high quality and great ingenuity. She has convinced a high proportion of the masses on Freeway that she is capable of a wide assortment of miracles, and this conviction is causing massive defections of the people of Freeway from their establishment culture. The government feels it can't be allowed to go on, and has asked for help—which is perfectly within their rights."

There was a long silence, while the Dean looked at him, and then she said, "What makes you so sure she is a fake, Alvin?"

STAR ANCHORED, STAR ANGERED

by

Suzette Haden Elgin

DAW BOOKS, INC.

DONALD A. WOLLHEIM, PUBLISHER

1633 Broadway, New York, NY 10019

First DAW Printing, May 1984

1 2 3 4 5 6 7 8 9

 DAW TRADEMARK REGISTERED
U.S. PAT. OFF. MARCA
REGISTRADA. HECHO EN U.S.A.

PRINTED IN U.S.A.

Chapter One

Even when the evidence had become overwhelming, supported by so many sets of statistics and so many superbly motivated arguments that there was no ground left to stand on, teachers refused to accept the obvious truth—that they were not needed in the classroom. With the perfection of inexpensive two-way cable television in the 1970s even their baby-sitting function ceased to have value. The sad result was the infamous Teachers Riots of 2002, in which hundreds of teachers and administrators died and thousands more suffered serious injury.

(It is of course important to remember that "teacher," as it was used during the Industrial Age of Old Earth and well into the beginning of the Electronic Age, did not have in any but the most general sense the meaning that we give the word "Teacher" today.)

> —*Encyclopedia Galactica*
> Fifth Edition, Volume V, p. 1134

Harvard was so exceedingly small an asteroid that its curvature was obvious at all times. Like standing on a well-landscaped billiard ball. Coyote was not quite willing to admit that it made him nervous; on the other hand, in spite of all scientific adjustments that eliminated sensations of motion, equalized gravity, and generally kept the thing suitable for *Planet & Asteroid*, he had the uncomfortable sensation that it ought to be easy to fall off of. The trees, for

5

example, had a decided tilt. Those at a distance tilted *away* from him.

"This world," he said to nobody, "is not flat. It is round." As was of course true of all worlds with which he was familiar, but on none of the others had he longed for a safety line.

The Student who had come up behind him must have been used to this reaction. He greeted Coyote from a distance obviously intended not to startle the already-uneasy visitor.

"After a day or two, Citizen Jones," he said soothingly, "you get used to it and it seems just as big as any other place you've ever lived. All a matter of perception, you know."

"I find that hard to believe," Coyote grumbled. He grabbed his beard, for want of anything else to hold on to, and tugged at it ferociously.

"It's true, though," said the Student, smiling at Coyote as his visitor turned—carefully—to face him. "Unfortunately, since your visit is to be so brief, you won't have a chance to put my claim to the test."

"You're a kind of official greeting committee," Coyote said.

"A committee of one, Citizen. Here to welcome you to Multiversity Two. May your visit be productive."

Coyote had discovered that there was a certain angle, just beyond the Student's shoulder, at which he could fix his eyes without being able to see the horizon. He looked fixedly at the spot and tried smiling back.

"It's all right to be scared, you know," said the Student gently. "People always are. Why don't we go indoors where you can be more comfortable?"

"How much more . . . outdoors . . . is there?"

The Student waved a vague arm to the left, then to the right. "Just a park," he said. "A small waterfall, run by solar energy. An artificial lake for swimming. A few gardens."

Coyote braced himself, took his eyes away from the security spot, and looked around. Trees. Flowering hedges. Paths leading away, all leading downhill, under more trees. Wildflowers, mostly Old Earth varieties so far as he could tell, waving in tilted banks of purple, white, and gold.

"It's pretty," he said. "Prettier than Mars-Central. But I think you need guard rails all around it."

The Student grinned. "You'll come inside, then?"

Coyote nodded. "Please."

Ahead of them was a half-circle of large domes, connected by a tubular corridor, all of it the blinding white of pyroceramic, and relieved by no decoration whatsoever. Whoever had designed this institution of learning had not wanted anyone to be confused by its appearance.

"This," said the Student, leading the way toward the nearest of the domes, "is the College of Religious Science. There are one hundred and thirty Students living here."

"Why so many?"

The Student shrugged. "Religious Science is a popular major right now," he said.

"Any special reason for that, you think?"

He smiled, and Coyote realized that he was a very handsome young man in spite of the bizarre outfit—consisting entirely of pseudo-tattoos—that he was wearing. It wasn't easy to disregard the dozens of tattoos of yellow roses the Student had seen fit to apply to his person . . . wreaths and garlands and swags and sprays of them, complete with leaves, thorns, and tastefully executed bees. The fact that his skin was a rich dark brown helped; Coyote assumed that white-skinned Students stuck to red roses. Out of the small spray that circled the Student's eyes and trailed artistically down his nose and over his chin looked a fine honest face, with brown eyes, a good mouth, and high strong cheekbones. All hidden among the foliage.

"Fads in majors come and go," he was saying. "Just like they do in anything else."

"Clothes, for example," Coyote observed, following him along the corridor that circled the domes.

"Clothes?"

"Mmhmm."

"You should see some of the others."

"What?"

"If you think I'm strangely dressed, Citizen, you should see some of the others."

"It doesn't bother you to have a bee crawling up your penis?"

"What bee?"

Coyote pointed.

"That's only a tattoo, Citizen, it's not alive."

Coyote shuddered. "It would make me nervous," he said, and was rewarded by hearty laughter that indicated to him what a funny fellow *he* was. Him and his conservative navy blue loincloth. *With* a narrow white pinstripe.

He couldn't decide exactly what he thought of this corridor they were following. It showed no signs of the reckless expenditure of taxpayers' money that had been mentioned to him in his briefing for this mission. Bare synthowood floors, and rather poor imitations of washed pine, if he was any judge. Light globes suspended in suitable places. Banks of plants, an occasional sculpture flickering in a niche. Nothing ostentatious. Nothing to indicate that this was the dwellingplace of hundreds of the most brilliant citizens of the Three Galaxies.

"Where is the Dean's office?" he said abruptly, tearing his eyes away from a mobile that seemed determined to turn his head inside out. "I'd like to get this over with."

"Certainly, Citizen Jones," the Student said. "Follow the corridor on round, and you'll come to Room Thirty-nine—that's Citizen Dean O'Halloran's quarters. She's expecting you."

"Thank you, Citizen Student."

"Not at all. I'm pleased to have met you—it's not every day, after all, that one meets a specialist in Twentieth-Century Ballads."

"The Dean has wide interests," said Coyote carefully, and was rewarded with an enthusiastic nod from his guide.

"I wonder . . ." said the Student.

"Yes?"

"Could I ask you a personal question?"

"There still are some?" Coyote's eyebrows went up, and he waited, but he kept on walking.

"Is it true that you own a guitar made of real Old Earth wood, Citizen Jones? That's what they told us, but Student news sources are not always as trustworthy as they might be."

"It's true," said Coyote. "My guitar is rosewood. Real rosewood, not synthowood."

"Ah," sighed the Student. "Now, that's impressive. That *is* impressive. Perhaps some of us could see it later, when you've finished speaking with the Dean. Or perhaps you don't have time . . ."

Coyote shrugged. "If you want to see it," he said, "just go look. It's in my flyer, in a case behind the pilot's seat. Be careful, though."

"Just like that?"

"Well? Are you likely to destroy it as a protest against the eating of pork on Blythe-6 or something of that kind?"

The blossoms and leaves leaped around the young man's eyes, registering his outrage spectacularly. "Certainly *not*," he snapped.

"Then please help yourself," said Coyote. "And your friends as well. Carefully."

The Student actually bowed. Coyote hadn't seen anyone bow since he had had the good fortune to leave the planet Abba, that bastion of sexism and antiquated etiquette, for the last time. But he managed to bow back, and continued toward #39. The Student did seem to him to be a little odd, but not as odd as the articles in the news would have you believe. And, so far as that went, if you knew that you were one of the elitist of all elite, second in rarity only to the Communipaths themselves, one of one thousand chosen out of countless billions of prospects, surely you had a right to get a little scramble-brained about it. Common motif in Twentieth-Century Ballads was the rose-covered cottage; now we find ourselves with rose-covered Students. Time marches, of course, on.

The door of #39 had no palm-screen, no electronic eye, only a bare surface. He considered it a moment, and then knocked, at which it slid open without a sound. He stepped over the threshold and almost broke his neck.

Nobody, including the beflowered and bemannered Student, had bothered to warn him that there were three steps down to be negotiated on the other side of the door. Just like intellectuals to put steps in a place where there was no need for them and then cut a door high enough in the wall to justify their existence.

Still no sign of the fabled luxury. True, the walls were lined with thousands of microfilms and microfiche trays, but that could hardly be considered an extravagance here. The floor was covered with mats in a shabby synthostraw he hadn't seen in fifteen years; apparently the Dean was old-fashioned in her tastes. Or perhaps sensitive to the criticism about wasting tax revenues. And where, for that matter, *was* the Dean?

She came out of a window at the far end of the room, vaulting handily over its sill and extending a welcoming hand.

"Citizen Jones!" she boomed. He backed off a step. It was difficult to accept the small woman greeting him as the source of that enormous husky voice. And it was clear that Dean Shandalynne O'Halloran was old-fashioned about more than floor coverings, too; she apparently didn't concern herself with cosmetic injections. Since she wore not even a loincloth, it was vividly obvious that she sagged in all the places where women of her age had sagged in the past, before science liberated them from the gravitational effects of time.

"No," she said, "no, you're wrong."

"Mmmm," said Coyote.

"I've just been too busy," she assured him briskly. "Come the end of this term, I'll haul me off to the nearest urban medcenter and have my poor body renovated. I'm not totally indifferent to the shocking effects I have on the eye. . . . No, that's a lie. I take it back, Citizen Jones, I *am* totally indifferent. But people remind me. My Students, for instance, remind me. Faces like yours, when I meet a stranger, remind me."

"My dear Citizen Dean—"

She ignored him and dropped cross-legged to the mats beside a low table.

"A needle here, a needle there," she went on, oblivious to his discomfort, "and I'll look just like my granddaughters again. Which, I might add, is perfectly ridiculous."

"I didn't know they wore off," he fumbled.

"The cosmetic injections? Oh yes. You have to get them renewed every three years, or nature just takes its course. You don't think the powers that be would allow anything you only had to do once and for all, do you? Although I suppose circumcision does qualify that way. . . . But you know, if they could figure out a way to make the foreskin grow back so you had to go in twice a year for a trim, they would. Won't you sit down, Citizen?"

He joined her on the other side of the table, and was making a determined effort to look at the far corner of the room, when she reached across the bowl of fruit and took both his hands tightly in hers. He hadn't realized that breasts *drooped* like that, normally.

"Tell me, Citizen Jones," she said, holding his hands firmly so that he could scarcely follow his instincts to invent a pressing errand elsewhere, "don't your testicles droop? I mean, dear Citizen, would you expect them to charge on ahead of you, fully erect, making lumps in your clothing?"

Coyote closed his eyes and surrendered to his fate, and the silence grew all around them. It was a fair question, after all, and when he got back home again—assuming he ever did—he would take it up with his daughter. She had an excellent mind for this sort of thing. And then he felt his hands laid down for the useless objects that they were, and neatly arranged for him on the table, and he opened his eyes. She was looking right into them.

"Dear Citizen Jones," she said again, gently. "I've upset you. It comes of spending all my time with Students, who cannot, by definition, be upset. Perhaps we could begin all over again? We must just pretend that I did *not* greet you by flinging myself through a window at you stark naked, babbling all the while about my breasts and your testicles."

"It won't help," said Coyote sadly. "I could pretend. But you did do all that, you know."

"You couldn't just put it out of your mind?"

"No," said Coyote. "I don't think I could. I think we should just go on from here. Wherever here is."

The Dean sighed, and folded her hands in front of her. "I'll have to take a course or something," she said, frowning.

"Non-Students, Behavior With. I don't run into one of you people more than twice a year, you see, and generally when I do it's at some stupid state occasion where I have to wear what is offensively known as my Academic Regalia. And at which I *speak* in Academic Regalian. *Inter alia. Ad hoc. Cogito ergo sum. Hoc orbiter testes infinitum.*"

Coyote blinked. "I don't know the last one," he said.

"Of course not, I made it up. I am trying to put you at ease, in my own clumsy way—I do realize, you know, that whatever brings you here is a serious matter."

Still frowning, she produced a small file sheath, opened it and scanned it quickly, slapped it closed, and returned it to the niche under the table from which it had apparently come.

"Well, Citizen Jones," she said, and all banter was gone from her voice now, "I am advised that you have been authorized to go to the planet Freeway to investigate the current religious conflict there, and that you will be masquerading as a Student in Religious Science. I have also been authorized to give you all the help I can."

Coyote was reasonably certain that wasn't all she had to say, and he was right.

"Just exactly how did you manage all that?" she snapped, leaning toward him with both hands gripping the table between them. "It will be hundreds of years before Freeway is off Novice Planet status and required to give up its anti-tourist regulations—that's Point One. Point Two: nobody, but nobody, is allowed to 'masquerade' as a Student. Doesn't happen. And Point Three: just where do they come off, asking a Multiversity Dean to participate in this extravaganza?"

She was fairly spitting sparks at him, but Coyote was used to irritated officials. He felt considerably more comfortable now.

"The question of real interest, Citizen," he said, "is not how *I* managed all that—but how *you* were induced to agree to it."

"Standoff," said the Dean, and Coyote grinned at her.

"You must know someone very, very powerful," she said.

"As do you, Citizen Dean."

As she surely did, and no question about it. The eleven

Multiversity Deans had more power than any other group in the Three Galaxies. Not formally. Not in the sense that a government had power. But out of the Multiversities came the great judges, the scientists, the artists, the writers, all the intellectual and the political aristocracy; and every member of that aristocracy had a fanatical devotion to one or more of the Multiversity Deans. It was not a power to be lightly dismissed, and Coyote had the utmost respect for this chunk of a woman with the outsized voice.

"Very well, Citizen Jones," she said. "I won't torment you further. It's unbecoming of me, anyway, since you undoubtedly have orders you aren't allowed to ignore. Would you give me some sort of indication as to how we are supposed to proceed, then?"

Coyote relaxed, not that he gave a wafer-thin damn for his "orders." "I need to know how to pass as a Student of Religious Science. Or as a Student of anything, for that matter. I might add that I don't think much of this idea—I'm no intellectual, and no scholar, not by anyone's definition."

The Dean looked indifferent, both to his opinions and his protests.

"That's easy," she said. "Nothing to it. Please keep in mind, Citizen Jones, that out of all the billions and billions of people in the Tri-Galactic Federation, not one in ten thousand ever has been or ever will be in contact with a Student. Anything you do, therefore, so long as you *look* like a Student, should serve."

"You're sure of that?"

"Certain of it. Think of yourself; you've traveled from one end of the inhabited universe to the other, you're far more knowledgeable than the average citizen. Have you ever been in contact with a Student? Before arriving here today, that is."

"Never."

"Well, then, you see, nothing could be simpler to bring off. Once your costume is corrected, there are only two essentials. First, you have to be able to carry on a reasonably intelligent conversation if you meet someone whose educational specialty—not as a Student, of course, but through the edcomputers—has been the study of Religion.''

"That's not going to be easy."

"Why not?" asked the Dean. "Why ever not?"

"Because I know nothing about the subject, Citizen Dean. The Mass-Eds gave up on me early."

"Nonsense. It's merely a matter of tailoring *your* so-called specialty to something you do know well. Now . . . in your file I see that you spent a year in a Maklunite Cluster. Correct?"

"I turned out to be one of the worst Maklunites of all time. They had to throw me out."

"But you spent a year there."

"Sure. I wanted—I wanted *very* much to stay."

"What matters," said the Dean, making a vague gesture with both hands, "is that you can actually qualify as an expert on the Maklunite sect, you have actually lived among them, done fieldwork compatible with your Religious Anthropology undergraduate major. You need only go on and on about the Maklunite religion, you see. No one will expect you to know about others."

Coyote whistled. "Is that how it's done?" he teased.

She stiffened. "Certainly not!" she said disgustedly. "This is not how it is *done*, Citizen, this is how it is *faked*."

She reached under the table again and pulled out a microfiche packet. "This," she said, tapping it softly against the table, "is a selection of abstracts, prepared by me personally, from all the basic texts that you would have been expected to read as an undergraduate in Religious Anthropology and a graduate Student in Religious Science. You won't learn anything from them, but you will acquire the necessary names, dates, titles and so on . . . enough information to keep you from making a total ass of yourself so long as you are speaking only to amateurs. Should you, by some freak of fate, find yourself confronted by an expert, become ill. Faint. Fall off a parapet. All clear?"

Coyote took the sheath from her and slipped it into his pouch. "I'm grateful, Citizen," he said, and he meant it.

"And your Bureau, whatever its benighted identity may be, is presumably also grateful?"

Coyote all but batted his lashes at the lady. "Where," he asked blandly, "do you get these strange ideas? Perhaps you need a vacation from your duties."

She snorted, a sound that came from somewhere around her ankles and expanded in magnitude as it worked its way up.

"Then," she said, "there is the second crucial matter. You're going to Freeway—it says in your file—to complete your doctoral dissertation, in which you are going to compare the Maklunites to the religious rebels on Freeway."

"I am going to do that?"

"It says so, right here." She pointed under the table, where the source of all these things she kept materializing was presumably located.

"That's all very well—"

"Very simple," she said, cutting him off with a wave of her hand. "Let us consider the situation, as you would have considered it. You in your role of graduate Student in Religious Science, that is. On the one hand we find the Maklunites, a kind of splinter religious movement dedicated to a set of principles running counter to the mainstream of contemporary society. On the other hand, on Freeway we find a similar splinter movement, led by one Drussa Silver and calling themselves Shavvies. Superficially they share many, many similarities. The same love ethic. The same contempt for material goods. The same renunciation of technology. Et cetera, et cetera."

"But—"

The Dean raised one finger beside her cheek in the ancient gesture of Teachers, and he stopped.

"*However*," she continued, "although the Maklunites have spread throughout the Three Galaxies, establishing their Clusters far and wide, they have had little or no effect upon the cultures of the Federation. The Shavvies, on the contrary, although confined to a single small and backward Novice Planet, are about to bring the culture of *that* planet crashing down about them."

She stared at him, and he considered the possibility that he was expected to say something significant and stared over her head. It was rude, no doubt, but it was self-defense.

"Curiously," she said then, "nobody cares about the Maklunites. Let them spread to the outermost of the Extreme Moons . . . no one pays any attention. Their compulsion for service is, in fact, a great convenience. But let the Shavvies threaten turmoil on one poor little planet, and what happens?"

She struck the low table a blow with her fist that overturned the bowl of fruit and set apples and pears and some varieties he didn't even recognize rolling across the floor.

"What happens," she hissed, "is that this is taken so seriously that pressure is brought to bear on me—on *me*, Citizen Coyote Jones!—to help you stop Freeway's piddling little religious commotion!"

There was nothing at all that he could say, of course, and in such circumstances he had learned long ago to rely on silence. He felt the tickling sensation above and just back of his right eye that meant the Dean was trying mindspeech, and he carefully maintained a face meant to convince her that he felt nothing at all. It wasn't much of an exaggeration, since she could have kept that up for hours and the tickling would have been all the communication that took place.

The shadows were reaching across the floor toward them, through the open windows, and the sky was full of moons, real and faked. He could smell a heavy flower scent, but could not identify it.

"*Your* special skill, Citizen Jones," she said finally, "must be an ability to simply wait."

When that provoked no response, she sighed heavily and went on.

"Your specialty," she said, "is the effect of religion on cultures. Your dissertation topic is an explanation of this curious difference in effect between the Maklunites, whom you really know about, and the Shavvies, whom you are there to investigate."

He was beginning to see it clearly now, and he was pleased.

"It will work," he said, nodding his head. "I wouldn't have thought it was possible, but I believe it will work.

You're as much the strategist as they say you are, Citizen Dean.''

"It will work," she said grimly, in no way impressed with his little compliments, "so long as your tattoos are right."

"What tattoos?"

"Your pseudo-tattoos, my friend! They must be right."

"I don't have any."

"They're not marked into the skin like a real tattoo," she said impatiently, "they're just held by static electricity. You have no reason to look as if I'd suggested ritual mutilations."

"You really feel they're necessary?"

The Dean sat bolt upright and stared at him, eyebrows at maximum elevation.

"My poor Citizen," she said, "without tattoos you haven't a prayer of passing as a Student, no matter what my strategic skills on your behalf. People know nothing else about Students except the fairy tales they read in news bulletins, but they do know that they cover themselves with *tattoos*. I'll choose them myself . . . I can imagine what you'd do. One blue diamond in mid-chest, or something equally preposterous. I'll have a Student bring us a selection, as well as something to eat and drink."

Coyote was surprised. "The Students do that kind of thing themselves?"

"Why? Did you think they didn't? Who do you suppose does the work around here?"

"Not the Students, surely."

"Ah, but yes it *is* the Students—surely. Most surely. They do almost everything, so long as they are here. If they didn't, we'd be developing elitists, who would then take their elitism into our governments, our ed-programs, our hospitals, and our arts—and that would not do. History has ample evidence as to where *that* leads." She reached up to push a stud on the wall behind her head, and he saw her eyes flicker briefly in open mindspeech, presumably with someone better at it than he was.

"It won't take long," she said. "Among the skills we develop here is efficiency."

Coyote pulled a big cushion from a pile of them set against

a near wall, and made himself more comfortable, pleased that she did not see fit to bring in any lights to supplement the moons. Certain muscles of his body responded to the rearrangement with pleasure, and he smiled a general sort of smile, aimed at all things within radius.

"It's nice here," he said. "I like it. *Inside*, I like it. Outside, I dislike it very much."

The Dean chuckled. "Most people do at first," she said.

"You have real Teachers here?" Coyote asked lazily, making polite conversation while they waited. "Live ones?"

"Of course."

"Real ones, like they had back in the days before the Education Riots. Standing at the front of a room before a bunch of Students, talking."

"Yes," she said, "just like that. How does that strike you? Would you like to make an impassioned speech against the practice?"

"Do you hear a lot of those?"

"Certainly. 'Damned waste of the taxpayers' money! Archaic anachronism!' 'Let's put *everybody* on the edcomputers and use the Multiversities for . . .' I don't know. I think grain warehouses was the suggestion I heard most recently."

"But you don't think you're wasting money."

"Have another of those pillows, Citizen Jones," said the Dean. "The blue ones are the most comfortable. No. No, I don't think we are wasting money. I think that what we do here is more important than anything else done, anywhere else, by anybody else, in all the known universe. Does that answer your question?"

A soft "Ping!" behind him spared him from trying to achieve a suitable reply. A tall pitcher appeared, amber in the moonlight and beaded with frost, and a basket of hot sandwiches. Eating utensils, napkins, mugs . . . and a long, narrow mysterious box. The Student responsible for it all was gone with a speed that reminded him of the way the Dean whipped files in and out.

"You see?" she said. "Efficient, as promised. Help yourself."

"Citizen Dean, is that beer?" he asked hopefully.

"Certainly." The Dean poured them each a full tall mug. "Only beverage fit to drink anymore, to my mind," she said. "Synthetic wines . . . phaugh . . . enough to make a person gag. You like beer?"

Coyote rubbed his hands together, lifted the mug, took a long, cold draught, and let his face speak for him. Bliss. He was a happy man.

"Look at these, Citizen," the Dean was saying. "Aren't they spectacular?"

She was holding out the mysterious box to him, open now, and he looked into it curiously. The pseudo-tattoos that filled it were packed in layers between sheets of static-resistant clear plastic, and there was quite an assortment of them.

"I'm keeping the loincloth," he said firmly, "and this is a *very* good sandwich."

"Glad you like it—it's one of our best. Mostly protein, it can be fixed in two minutes flat, and it doesn't spill all over you when you're studying. The perfect sandwich. However, as to the loincloth—"

"I'm keeping it," he said. "I mean that. And I'll have no insects crawling up my penis, or snakes twining round it, or flowers blossoming out of the tip. My anatomy gets quite enough attention all on its own, without working at making it conspicuous. And my loins, dear Citizen Dean, are going to be girded up with conservative navy blue *cloth*, as always. No garlands of posies."

"Dear me, but you're vehement about it," she said mildly, looking at him over the edge of her beer.

"I am that," he agreed. "I surely am."

"Very well, then, we'll have to do something to offset the conservatism. Stand up, please."

And she proceeded to do him up, head to foot, as a Pokka Flame-tree. Orange roots wound round his ankles and feet and disappeared under his soles, silver-and-white-striped bark wound round his arms and legs, and despite the interference of his heavy beard and moustache, she managed to add at least a dozen scarlet blossoms. The crowning touch was a pita-bird, colored like the rainbow, perched over his left eyebrow.

Coyote looked at himself with disgust and said a few words on the subject, but the Dean was adamant.

"Do you want to look like a Student, Citizen Jones, or don't you?" she demanded.

"Do you realize," he grumbled, "how *easy* it would be to pass yourself off as a Student? Easiest blooming—and I do mean blooming—disguise in the Three Galaxies!"

"Mmmmm . . . not so easy as you think. Not without help."

"Why not?"

"Up until the first time you tried to use your credit disc, or any other kind of identification, you'd be all right. At that precise moment the Central Computers would punch in for an electronic roll call of all Students, and all of a sudden there'd be one thousand and *one*, and the other thousand all accounted for."

"At which point?"

"At which point Fedrobots would come from more directions than you were aware existed. At a speed . . . oh, roughly that of narrow light. And you'd be in one of the biggest troubles there is, Citizen."

Coyote frowned, set down his sandwich and his beer, and opened his mouth to speak, but she raised that finger again and stopped him.

"In your case," she said, "in your very special and mysterious case, the computers have been reprogrammed to accept you. You'll have no trouble, Coyote Jones—no trouble at all."

When the man had gone, armed with all the vocal information she had been able to provide in so short a time, plus a microxerox of her own copies of Shavvy rituals and sacred documents, and the file of basics, Dean O'Halloran sat by her window watching the trees cast patterns across the sloping lawns of Harvard. The problem she faced was anything but academic.

She had more than enough power to do whatever she wanted; that wasn't the difficulty. The difficulties were two-fold. First, she had no idea why Coyote Jones was being sent to Freeway, and she had good reason to be distressed about that gap in her knowledge. The second difficulty was more abstract: how was she to fit what she felt must be done into the framework of what her religious convictions would allow her to do? Having Coyote Jones shot, which appealed to her in a way she found shocking, was clearly not the solution. Stopping him from reaching Freeway—stopping him completely—was clearly impossible, given the lofty source of the pressure being exerted to send him there. Violence was forbidden to her no matter what she planned, and complete inaction was not within the bounds of her own tolerance.

As was her habit in such situations, she made lists. Lists of the problems, lists of the possible solutions—ranked for their varying degrees of outrageousness—lists of the steps necessary to effect those solutions, and lists of the advantages and disadvantages of each. It took a little time, but when she got to the end of the process, she had answered her own questions.

Delay. Delay required no violence—only interference—and she had at her disposal an assortment of ways to create delays. Virtually endless delays, if that should prove necessary. And it might. She needed time to find out what sort of danger the man represented. He was handicapped; that was certain. She had tried half a dozen times to reach him by mindspeech and it had been like addressing a wall, or a rock. And yet, if he had not been special in some way, he could not have been sent to take part in this venture . . . which was what?

But she would have to move quickly now. Very quickly. The liner with Coyote Jones aboard, suitably disguised as a Student in all his horticultural glory, would be docking at Phoenix-One within three hours. Unless she could manage to wangle a long period of circling in orbit, a longer wait for landing clearance, perhaps a bit of trouble with the landing mechanisms that nobody would be able to locate for quite a while . . .

The Dean spent five more minutes putting together another list; this time it was a list of names. Then she went to her comset and began making calls.

Chapter Two

Once a stewardess out walking
Thought she heard a Waker talking;
Off she ran to see her Shrink,
Didn't even stop to think

What a fool her tongue would make her
Since she couldn't *speak* in Waker.
Said the wise psychiatrist:
"What can't be said does not exist."

—Ancient Freeway jumprope
rhyme

At the Castles the Wakers were on duty, stationed on the balconies outside the sleeping-rooms of the noble families, their metal sensors quivering above the tight-shut purple bells of the dawnflowers. When the flowers folded back their petals, sending up golden-flecked central clusters and releasing their honey-and-rose fragrance on the air, the Wakers would sound the morning tone and wake the families.

The dawnflowers never made a mistake. Often on Freeway it poured torrents of rain in the early morning, but the flowers knew, always, when somewhere beyond the thick cloud cover the light made its first tentative move across the sky and day began to break. The flowers knew even before it happened; when exactly one-half of a one-hundred-minute Freeway hour remained before first dawn, the flowers opened, leaving the families time to bathe and dress and reach their Chapels by the exact moment of daybreak.

It would have been more economical, and therefore more pleasing to each Castle's Economist, if the flowers could have been made to issue the warning themselves, without the supplement of the Wakers. Many things had been tried along this line, all the way from an attempt at amplification of the almost soundless sound of the unfolding petals—a tactic which had only killed the flowers—to a trial at actually training the flowers. Certainly every Citizen in the Castles was capable of picking up the mindvoices of the blossoms, soft as they were, if their distance from the human ear was reduced enough. But this had failed as well, despite its plausibility. The dawnflowers had stubbornly refused to cooperate. (Or perhaps it wasn't stubbornness. There was no way of knowing whether they had understood what was wanted of them.) It had been necessary to keep the cumbersome Wakers, expensive as they were to maintain, and a constant burden on the Castle budgets.

In the bedrooms the nobility lay in their sleeping-slots, layer upon layer according to their rank, breathing air piped into the drawers and carefully monitored by the central computer. The air for sleeping was a public utility, and a necessity if one were to avoid the narcotic blandishments the giant ferns released upon the night air of the planet. A certain limited immunity had been built up in the people, of course, after all these years, and a Citizen who was awake could not be distracted by the drugged air. But now and again someone caught outside the buildings fell asleep during the night despite all efforts to remain awake, and the resulting disorientation of the mind was said to be incurable. No prudent Citizen chanced exposure, and the most terrifying threat a bullying older child could make to a young one was, "I'll come in after you're asleep and put you OUTSIDE, you little twit!"

In the top rank of the innermost bedchamber of Castle Fra the child Deliven lay awake, ahead of the Wakers. It was her habit to wake early, long before the others, and it was her burden as well, because it was boring in the sleeping-slots. They were like long shallow drawers; seven feet long, five feet wide, and just under four feet deep. Just enough room for copulation, should desire strike in the middle of the night—a rare occurrence among the nobles, whose administrative schedules kept them so busy that they were exhausted by bedtime. And for a small child the slots were not overly unpleasant. Deliven could remember a time when she was smaller, when it had been almost like being in a playhouse; you could move around inside and pretend that you were a spaceliner captain or that you were in a treecave, you could take your dolls or your painting sticks to bed the night before, and there was room to play with them in the morning. But Deliven was growing. She was unusually tall for her twelve years, and she could no longer move about freely in the sleeping-slot. She could only lie and wait for the Wakers to call, since it was strictly forbidden to rise until they did.

She thought a great deal in these early mornings before the Wakers released her. Thought took up no room and it required no movement, though perhaps inside the head things were moving. The edcomputers had once shown her a threedy of a thinking brain, the silver sparks showering at the synapses, the exquisitely thin boundaries of the brain cells flashing as the thought leaped from neuron to neuron. For weeks afterward she had walked cautiously, painfully conscious of the activity, like traffic in the city streets, inside her small skull, almost afraid to shake her head. Until the new knowledge had worn off and become background, like her knowledge of her throbbing heart and racing blood.

She would lie and think of her mother, a woman broad-shouldered and broad-hipped like all the women of her family, strong as any man and yet gentle with her children, and of the trouble that was sure to come when she, Deliven, began to rebel against that gentle control. As she *would* have to, of course. She would think, too, of her arrogant father, whose unthinking callous touch in the government was certain to bring disaster down upon Castle Fra one of these days. When her mother had stepped down from her post as Sector Governor, turning it over to her husband in order to be free for a life of study and research, there had been a lot of talk that she should be forced to reassume the position. Only a few days had had to go by before the Citizens saw what a poor substitute they had in Bardow Kellyr. But Deliven's mother had ignored them, plunged herself even deeper into her work, and had let her husband's natural talent for blundering take its course.

"He will *learn*, Citizens," she had said, looking up grudgingly from her microviewer at the committee come to call on her. "He will learn. You must be more patient, and less demanding."

"Citizen Kellyr," the committee chair had snapped, "we demand only that you do your duty."

Tayn Kellyr had raised beautiful dark brows long enough to say, "My duty is to my self, Citizen, I have filled my allotted term in service to the state," and no amount of persuasion or apology on their parts would draw another word from her. And so things had gone from bad to worse in the Sector.

When Deliven remembered what had happened yesterday, her cheeks grew hot and the patterns on the sleeping-slot roof above her squirmed before her eyes. The boy her father had slapped had meant no harm. He was young and inexperienced, and his hold on the Chapel bellropes had been faulty only because he was frightened. So minor a violation of the holy ritual . . . what deity could object to one careless extra stroke of a bell? But Bardow Kellyr had gone in heavy swift strides to the back of the Chapel and laid a blow across the boy's face without a single word, leaving an angry welt for his parents to watch grow redder all through the morning service.

That her father was under a strain, sick with worry about the numbers lost each day from the Castles and from the Old Faith to the Shavvies was no excuse. That was not the boy's fault. The problem was that there seemed to be no way to stop the flood of Citizens from defecting. Even before the first starships had left Earth to seed the Inner Galaxy, religious persecution had disappeared from the patterns of human behavior. Bardow Kellyr was not such a fool as to think he could revive the barbaric customs of thousands of years ago. And yet he needed desperately to strike out at someone— something—and his powerlessness galled him unmercifully. Striking the boy had no doubt been a relief.

Deliven had seen her mother's face stiffen when the sound of the slap broke the Chapel hush, and she had seen Tayn Kellyr take a small note-fiche from her pocket and mark it swiftly with her stylus. She had looked at her husband in a different way when he returned to their pew at the front of the Chapel, a measuring way that brought a first tentative hope to the watching Deliven. Perhaps now her mother would see the seriousness of the situation and do something about it. This was more than a mistake in the programming of water allocations, or a clumsy joke that violated someone's family taboos, or a failure to answer an official communication by its due date. What Bardow Kellyr had done was a serious and shameful matter—an offense to another noble family—for the boy had been visiting their Chapel with his parents, and he had been given the bellringing task as an honor.

There would be a formal complaint, of that Deliven was sure. She kicked fretfully at the top of her sleeping-slot; would it never be time to get up? This morning, in the Sector Gallery, the boy's parents would make a formal charge. They were Cadys, a proud family, conservative beyond the usual degree and sensitive to insult. They would be there with a formal Petition of Injury when the judges opened the Gallery, and Deliven was reasonably sure that during the night they had made a journey to speak to one of the judges in advance of the opening. She had heard a flyer leave the Castle shortly after midnight, and she had not heard it return.

There would be stories in the news-sheets, and probably demonstrations in the Cady Sector, demands that the pointless insult be compensated for. . . .

Deliven sighed. This religious problem was too much for her fumbling father to handle. Three years ago, when her mother had stepped down from the governorship, there had been only a handful of these people who called themselves Shavvies, living out at the fringes of the planet. A few hundred here, a few hundred there, following a set of absurd and naïve rituals in their so-called holy book, repudiating the Old Faith and waiting for their promised Messiah to take up the leadership of their number.

Messiah! It was common rumor, among the noble families,

that this "Messiah" had been a Fealtor's child, daughter of a widower working at the lowest of Freeway trades—a scavenger, supervising the robot Sweepers and Suckers. It was said that she had been intended as a tiringmaid to a noblewoman, and if that was true she would have to have come from the Sector of Castle Bernadette of Pau. Only in that most antiquated of Sectors would a woman allow herself to be considered an idiot unable to dress without assistance.

Things were very different now. Wherever Drussa Silver had come from, she was drawing the best and the finest of their people away from the Castles, drawing them away from the Old Faith, sapping the strength of the nobility and leaving it only the weak, the old, and the foolish, like Bardow Kellyr.

It made Deliven uneasy to know so little of the facts about the woman. She felt it her obligation to be informed of every detail of possible political significance; it was her responsibility to do so. After all, if anything were to happen to her father, it would be Deliven who had to take over the reins of Sector government. Her mother would never go back to the governorship again.

For her father to behave as he was behaving, forbidding Deliven to watch the newscasts or read the news-sheets about this fabled woman of miracles and wonders, was foolish. She ignored his instructions, as she ignored his bellowing that the woman was a "devil, a demon, a pestilence, a *disease!*" who destroyed the people and their lives with her sorceries. Her younger brothers were impressed when he called the woman a venomous reptile and swore that her name was not to be spoken in the Castle, but Deliven was not. And her mother just sat, saying nothing, allowing the nonsense to continue. . . . Deliven was disgusted with her, too. Bad enough for her father to behave like an idiot—he *was* an idiot; her mother had no such excuse.

Her youngest brother had asked timidly if it were true that the woman now had more than three million followers, and that half of them had come from the Castles in the past three years, from the noble families themselves and from the Fealtors.

"Lies!" Bardow Kellyr had bellowed. "Lies! A handful of

rubble only—parasites on society—and none of those from the noble families. They come from the lowest classes—remember that!''

Now *that* was a lie. Deliven knew that, as did everyone else in the Castle, including her father, and lies do not change the truth. The truth was that the trickle of converts had become a torrent, that every day another of the great dancing-circles ringed with giant ferns and floored with four-foot-broad planks from the nishia-bella trees turned up in the forests of Freeway. The sound of the Shavvy axes and saws, building them, the slap of the trowels laying the central spirals of emerald-green tiles in the center of the dancing-circles, could be heard from every window. They used hand tools. Hand tools! In the thirty-first century, when such things were seen only in the back rooms of museums. Deliven chuckled, thinking of it, amused at such childishness. The Chapels of the Old Faith were built by computer, just as were the Castles, and they were certainly holy. The idea that a holy place must be built entirely by hand! Such superstition . . .

The call of the Waker cut across her thought, and she sighed again, but this time with relief. Now the day could begin. Whatever it might bring, at least it could begin. She opened the front-leaf of her sleeping-slot, and heard the soft click as the piped air was cut off by the Central Computer.

II

The Head called the roll of the Council of Eight, noting with approval that everyone had managed to reach the meeting by the hour designated, in spite of the short notice they had been given.

"Castle Fra."

"Present." Tayn Kellyr gave the Head one swift glance and went back to her microviewer.

"Castle Able."

"Present."

"Castle Tenasselle."

"Present."

"Castle Hight."

"Present."

"Castle Olyon."

"Present."

"Castle Bernadette of Pau."

"Present."

"How can you answer to that silly name?" the Head demanded, as he did at each and every meeting. "When are you going to change it to something that doesn't make everybody snicker? Bernadette of Pau, indeed . . . why not Marianne of Topeka, or Epsomia of Salts?"

He was ignored as always, Félice Manoux-Gerardain not even bothering to respond. The citizens of Castle Bernadette of Pau were passionately proud of the ancient name and would keep it despite all his teasing.

"Castle Helix."

"Present."

"And I," finished the Head, "sit for Castle Guthrie. We are all here, then, and right on the hour. I appreciate your speedy cooperation."

Nicol Asodelyr tugged at his long black braid and glared at their presiding officer. "You had better have a good and sufficient reason to have brought us here," he said sharply. "I have three rivers at floodpoint in my Sector, my Chief Fealtor was injured in a ridiculous accident with a servomechanism yesterday, and this is a poor time for me to be away from Castle Hight."

The Head smiled at him. "Not only is it an excellent reason, my good Citizen Asodelyr," he said, "but we should not be here more than perhaps twenty minutes."

"All this fuss for twenty minutes?" Asodelyr struck his forehead with the heel of his hand. "Absurd!"

From across the table, Tayn Kellyr looked up from her microviewer and frowned.

"What would you have suggested that we do in order to give you our news, Citizen Asodelyr?" she murmured. "Perhaps a comset announcement?"

"I simply—"

"You know quite well," she went on, cutting him off,

"that it is not safe for the Council of Eight to transmit any information whatsoever—no matter how brief, or seemingly trivial—by any means other than face to face contact. We deplore as much as you do the necessity for all this melodramatic junketing about in caves and tree trunks; nonetheless, it is essential if we are to preserve our secrecy."

Asodelyr lowered his eyes, rebuked into silence, and the Head moved to fill the awkward silence. There were times when he wished that Tayn Kellyr could find a little more tolerance for the foibles of others in her heart, although conceivably such a tolerance might diminish her usefulness.

"We have good news," he said quickly. "You should all be pleased."

"High time," said Donald Minora, representative of Castle Able. "We have put enough effort into this project, and enough years of work."

"We were fortunate to have had those years' warning, Citizen," said the Head. "Can you conceive of what our problems would have been had we not had all this time?"

"I can. I am not a fool," Minora snapped. "Now could we have the news? Or is this to be like the threedy newscasts, Citizen Begaye, with little feelers to build the suspense?"

Aaron Begaye sighed softly, wishing he were Head of almost anything but a council of eight superchiefs. Eight people accustomed to instant obedience from everyone around them, eight people who took their enormous power for granted. Too many to have in one room.

"Will you tell them, please, Citizen Kellyr," he said. "You are more familiar with the details, I believe, than anyone else here."

"Very well," said Tayn Kellyr. "It is a simple matter . . . the plan has at least begun its final stages. The TGIS agent, Coyote Jones, will arrive on Freeway in four days."

"Excellent!" said Bent Cady, of Castle Olyon. "That is welcome news, and I agree with Citizen Minora—it is high time."

"Until as recently as three weeks ago," Tayn Kellyr went on, "we were far from certain that the Tri-Galactic Council was going to accept our story. If they had not done so we could not have risked our plan—not with the proportion of our Citizens now defecting to the Shavvy cult.''

"That proportion," put in the Head, "had reached thirty-one per cent, as of dawn this morning, and of that thirty-one per cent almost a fifth comes from Castle families and high-ranking Fealtors."

Enaphel Smythe, representative of Helix, smacked the table with a powerful fist and swore.

"Only a week ago it was not yet at thirty per cent," he protested. "What is the matter with people, anyway?"

"Well," said Tayn Kellyr, "it is possible to understand the behavior of the Fealtors, I think. Part of their defection is our own fault for not being more generous with them—particularly in the southern Sectors—and they are given to superstition. The Silver's tricks appeal to them. But for our own people, I cannot explain this phenomenon at all. They are educated. They know that religion has almost nothing to do with spirituality and is simply a matter of economics, but they behave like children just hearing the Miracle Myths from the edcomputer. It baffles me . . . particularly in view of the practices of the cult."

"The repulsive practices," Smythe said, his face working with distaste. "Mauling about in one another's minds—"

The gavel was symbolic, and a symbolic relic at that, but Aaron Begaye hit the table with it anyway. He countenanced no salacious talk, no dirty allusions, in his presence—not even from men or women far gone in celebration. At a meeting like this he would tolerate not even a nuance.

"Sorry," muttered Enaphel Smythe. "I am sorry . . . but it is so disgusting."

"No need for you to be disgusting in return," said the Head firmly.

The representative from Castle Tenasselle leaned forward, reaching for a cup of tea from the center of the table, and spoke to Tayn Kellyr. "Do you think," she asked, "that this man is going to serve our purposes? After all, the Tri-Galactic Intelligence Service is hardly an ideal recruiting ground for dupes . . . at least one hopes that it is not."

"I do think so, Citizen Bass," said Tayn Kellyr. "He is

perfectly suited to our needs, he is basically an ignorant man, he is known to be given to emotional excesses of various kinds, and he is completely unaware that he is here for any purpose other than that explained to him by his superiors.''

"Emotional excesses . . .''

Tayn Kellyr shrugged. "He is excessively fond of women, I understand, and a perfect fool about children. Just the sort of person who might be taken in by the romantic nonsense the Shavvies deal in.''

"And if he becomes suspicious?''

"How could he?'' said the Head. "We have survived eighteen years on this planet without our own Citizens suspecting our existence. How should an offworlder become suspicious? Of course he won't; he will do what we intend him to do and nothing more.''

"Good,'' came the responses from around the room. "Excellent.''

Philomena Bass sipped her tea, still frowing, but she made no more protests, asking only, "What do you want us to do now, then? What steps shall we take?''

"Step up the pressure,'' said the Head flatly. "Make things worse. Create unrest. More incidents such as happened yesterday at Castle Fra. More young boys slapped for ringing the Chapel bell one too many times. That's what is needed. I cannot emphasize too strongly that it is absolutely necessary that the people, both noble and Fealtor, become more and more restless, more and more upset, about conditions in the Sectors. We cannot afford to have a single contented Citizen, if we are to succeed. They must become distressed enough to ensure that they will *welcome* the final outcome of our plan.''

"You exaggerate, Citizen Begaye,'' said Tayn Kellyr. "Our computers indicate that we can afford to have as high as thirteen per cent of the people uninvolved in all this.''

"It was a figure of speech, my dear cousin,'' said the Head.

"This is no time for rhetorical flourishes.''

"Agreed,'' said the Head wearily. "Please go on.''

"It was you who were talking, Citizen Begaye.''

"Ah, yes, I lose track at times, as I get older. Perhaps one of you others should take over the post of Head of this Council."

He waited, but no one offered. They all had better sense, and he only wished that eighteen years ago he had been similarly wise. It was a thankless post.

"Are there any questions?" he said finally. "Any leftover difficulties?"

"One question," said Philomena Bass. "Will it work?"

"Indications are that it has almost no chance of failing," said Tayn Kellyr. "We have moved so slowly. So carefully. Every contingency has been anticipated."

"You know what the loss of Old Faith tithes will do to us if this fails?"

Tayn Kellyr frowned at her. "If it fails," she said, "we shall move on at once to the backup plan next on our list of success-probables. Let us not become emotional."

"Your husband," said Enaphel Smythe, "is doing an excellent job. Never have I seen such a bumbler, such a clumsy tactless man, such a—well . . . what word is nearest to my meaning? . . . such a *perfect* example of an administrator. One thinks of the great Business Riots of 2989 . . ."

"As I recall," Tayn Kellyr observed, "it was for that precise reason that the Council chose Bardow as husband for me, fifteen years ago."

"He has surpassed our wildest dreams," said the Head. "It is astonishing that he escaped Reconditioning. Any other questions?"

There was silence around the table, and he nodded with satisfaction. He was as anxious to get home as any of them, and it was both damp and cold inside this tree.

"You know your role, then," he said. "Make trouble. Cause chaos. The TGIS agent must see evidence that he is really *needed* here, that his mission is real and not the panicky paranoia of a Novice Planet. He must be convinced that Drussa Silver is in fact destroying our society."

"Nonsense," snapped Asodelyr. "She's a nuisance, she's a blight, but destruction? If there's any paranoia about, Citizens, it's—"

"And," went on the Head loftily, sailing right over the top of Asodelyr's outraged complaining, "be prepared to be called back at any moment. We cannot know from one hour to the next what need there may be for action from the Council. All of us must stay close to home, easily reached. If you must supervise your Sectors, do so by comset, not in person. We are at the final stages now; nothing must be allowed to go wrong because of *carelessness*."

When they were all gone, in various stages of fuss and bother, the Head turned to Tayn Kellyr and touched her arm.

"We regret at times," he said gently, "the necessity that forced us to pair you off for life with that unpleasant man. If there had been any other way, we would have taken it."

"That's quite all right, Cousin Aaron," said Tayn, smiling. "It has been good for my character, all these years."

"It has made you hard, Tayn."

"Hard times," snapped the lady of Castle Fra, "call for hard persons. We use what comes to hand."

"And your children? What has it done to them?"

She pulled her robes tight around her, and settled the bulky hood about her face.

"The boys are young," she said. "It's too soon to speak for them. But my daughter Deliven . . . ah, there is a woman born to rule, Aaron! She is as utterly logical as a computer, and as immune to any emotional appeal. If she were called upon to take over the Sector tomorrow, she would do better than her father."

Aaron Begaye walked with her down through the tunnels cut in the great trunk, to the exit ramp hidden in the hillside against which the tree rose, and watched her leave. She took the flyer from the ramp to the highest level of the giant tree in seven seconds flat, as sure a hand at the flyer controls as she had always been at the controls of government.

It was sad. He could remember her as a girl, an almost plump young girl with immense dark eyes, and brown hair in a cap of short curls around her head. She had been fond of dolls and had refused to give them up until she was almost fourteen years old, as he recalled. He was not quite sure where that girl had hidden herself in the steel-and-whipcord woman who was—he was the first to admit it—truly the Head of the Council of Eight.

Chapter Three

The development of telepathic projection techniques was held back for almost a century by the powerful Grinder Psychoconglomerate, which dominated all psychological and social sciences until the last of the Orthodox Grinderian Karismatics was assassinated in 2064. Perhaps the most obstructive of all the Grinderian Postulates was the Fourth, which claimed that no human being could be harmed by the thoughts or emotions of any other human being. Humankind is indeed fortunate that this dangerous and seductive movement was at last brought to a halt, although no one can admire the violent act which was the first step toward its downfall.

—*Encyclopedia Galactica*
Fifth Edition, Vol. IV, p. 1421

For a while it had appeared that the liner *Lazyday* would never dock on Phoenix-One. Coyote had lost all count of the waiting orbits the ship had been obliged to maintain, and none of the coy placating techniques used by the liner staff had helped his bad temper in the slightest. He took no pleasure in seeing twenty-year-old threedies about intrepid colonists beating back helpless indigenous wildlife. Nor did he feel that heavily watered drinks served in edible mint-flavored tubes, or low-grade marijuana spiked with nutmeg, represented any kind of peak experience. There had been a bearable half-hour when one of the copilots had come to share his seat and tell him hair-raising stories about her early days on the Greyhound Rockets, but that had only made the boredom more painful when she moved on to the next passenger across the aisle.

By the time docking actually took place, he was cross and tired and disgusted. His head ached. His skin itched under the unaccustomed pseudo-tattoos. He was tired of the stares he was getting from the other passengers when they realized that they were sharing their liner with a real live Student. A furious baby had vomited down his back, bringing on a solicitous scrubbing down with ice water and Spotnomore by its embarrassed father.

He no longer saw himself, as the liner finally berthed, as the steely-eyed, red-bearded, musclebound secret agent off to do daring derring-do. He just wanted to go home to his daughter and help her water her plants, and maybe buy her a new gaza hound just because he had sworn that two such creatures was his limit.

He stumbled down the landing-ramp, muttering to himself and wondering what shape the next foul-up would take in this so-called mission. For example, there could be a note waiting to tell him that instead of his flyer being sent back from Harvard on automatic, per his instructions, it had mistakenly been tucked in with the cargo for a shipment to one of the Third Galaxy factories. For example, there could—

And then he saw the foul-up, right there before his eyes, and stopped worrying about the other possibilities. It was a vision of . . . something. Not loveliness. It stood well over six feet tall, had enough shoulders for two normal people, sported a wasp waist and black hair flowing down its back, and it had great bulging lumps all over it that had been, long ago perhaps, human muscles. And it was clearly waiting for him.

A *Jock*, bigawd. A fathering Jock. And a Student Jock, at that, which was something he hadn't known existed. It was done up in multicolored stars and pinwheels, and its testicles were a spectacular display all by themselves, what with the feathers, and the Catherine wheels, and the silver-and-gold ruffles. . . . Coyote went over to the side of the landing ramp, where he was in everybody's way, leaned on the ramp's invisible guard-rails, and stared fixedly off into the distance while the Student waved wildly. Maybe it would go away?

"Citizen," said the robostew at his elbow, "you are holding up the disembarkment of this flight. If you are ill, will you please signal by saying aloud I AM ILL. If you are not ill, will you please move on. Thank you, Citizen."

Coyote glared down at the top of the poor little thing, all dented plastic and burnt-out lights and punched-in speakers, and he just hadn't the heart to give it any more trouble. He moved on down the ramp, determined to charge right past the waving Student and on into the night, and then he changed his mind.

As he would have changed his mind about stopping if a brick wall had suddenly bumped up against his chest. He looked straight at the creature, his eyes level with its massive nose, and sighed.

"Citizen Jones," said the Student, "I have a message for you."

"So I assumed," said Coyote. He was doing Weary Secret Agent Assumes Sardonic Tone With Underling. When tired, he found this sort of capital-letter self-programming one of the better ways of staying on his feet and not disgracing himself.

"A message from Dean O'Halloran, Multiversity Two. She's gone to a lot of trouble to get it to you, Citizen."

"Well?"

"Well, what, Citizen?"

This was a Student? This was a member of the intellectual elite of the universe, selected by years of painstaking observation and batteries of subtle tests? Still crammed flesh-to-flesh with the young man, Coyote did the best he could to look flabbergasted, and the Student—finally—turned red under the stars and spangles and backed off.

"I beg your pardon, Citizen Jones," he said. "I was distracted by all the noise."

Coyote said nothing at all. Weary Secret Agent Signifies Mute Contempt For Underling.

"The message," said the Student, "is that Drussa Silver is

not on Freeway at this time and won't be there for several weeks. Dean O'Halloran wanted to be sure you would not waste time going there after her.''

Coyote took a deep breath, shoved past the Student to a nearby plastibench, sat down firmly, and said, ''Oh, putrescence!'' as clearly and vigorously as he could manage in his current state of exhaustion. ''Oh, *flowering* putrescence!'' he added for good measure.

''I *am* sorry,'' said the Student, sitting down beside him. The plastibench creaked alarmingly, and Coyote braced himself against its imminent collapse.

''What is your major, anyway?'' he asked the Jock.

''Music, Citizen.''

''Music?''

''Yes, Citizen. I'm a harpist.''

''A *what?*''

The Student looked miserable, and dogged, and said, ''Well, I am, you know. I play a harp. I play it very well, I compose for it, I am at the head of my classes.''

Coyote was genuinely curious now, and he asked gently, ''When did they let you know that you were going to be a Student?''

''Late. Very late.''

''I see.''

''See here, Citizen Jones, I really am sorry. They tell me you've been going around up there for hours. And it must be rotten to get down here, finally, and find out that your plans are all fouled up.''

''It's not your fault,'' said Coyote grudgingly. ''It would have been even worse if I'd gone on from here to Freeway and *then* found out the Silver wasn't there.''

''Your thesis depends on direct observation of Citizen Silver, then?'' said the young man, and Coyote nodded gravely.

''Oh yes,'' he said. ''Yes, indeed. And I could do with some more information. Did the Dean tell you where Citizen Silver is, if she's not on Freeway? Or has she ascended to the skies, to fall to earth we know not where . . . or something.'' He was overtired. He was definitely overtired.

"She has gone, I understand, with a group of Shavvies, on a missionary expedition to Galoralon."

"Oh, no." Coyote leaned back against the hood of the bench and closed his eyes.

"I know how you must feel," said the Student softly.

"No, you don't."

"I do," he insisted. "*Everybody* knows about Galoralon."

Coyote opened his eyes. "Why," he asked, "why would she want to go there, on a missionary or any other kind of expedition? Can you tell me that? It's the nether asshole of the universe, Galoralon. It's the Pesthole Expert's Pesthole. Even the bugs on Galoralon wish they could leave . . . not to mention the slime molds."

"Perhaps she felt that the people of Galoralon really needed her help, Citizen."

"Perhaps. Perhaps she is mad, as well as a fake." He closed his eyes again, and contemplated the blackness there, shot now and again by a gloating little yellow thing that slid across his eyeball and out of sight.

"Is she a fake, Citizen Jones?"

Coyote's eyes snapped open, and he glared at the Student.

"Well of course she is," he said crossly. "That's a ridiculous question."

"Well," said the Student, "Dean O'Halloran does not agree that she is a fake."

Oops. A small warning bell managed to get past the fog in Coyote's mind and recall to his attention the fact that one does not—repeat does *not*—attempt to alter the special kind of trust a Student usually has for Deans. It was just that Citizen O'Halloran had seemed so spectacularly pragmatic.

"Dean O'Halloran," he said musingly, watching the Student's face, "is a fine, intelligent woman. A bit behind on her cosmetic injections, perhaps, a bit too eager to race up and down halls and in and out the windows, but a fine, intelligent woman nonetheless. Not the sort to be taken in by a bag of cheap psi-tricks."

The Student's face assumed the thunderclouded aspect he was anticipating, and Coyote stood up immediately, obliging the young man to occupy himself in keeping the plastibench from falling over with him.

"Do you suppose I can get a visa for Galoralon?" Coyote asked, changing the subject.

The Student snickered. "I expect they *pay* people to visit Galoralon," he said. "I'll bet you can get visas for Galoralon out of the comsets, Citizen."

He turned out to be right. The official only grinned when asked about the visa, whipped out a stamp whose shining condition showed the rareness of its use, stamped Coyote's unipass with a resounding thwack, and stood there smirking at him.

"Have a pleasant visit," said the official, and Coyote smirked back.

"May your mother's breasts fall off," he said pleasantly.

He retrieved his luggage from the ejectislot in the far wall, disentangled himself from the Student, and went to the nearest hertz to rent a flyer. He was through with commercial flights, and the Service could bloody well pick up the tab for the rental. Enough was enough.

"You're leaving at once, Citizen?" carolled the rental robot.

"Certainly not," snapped Coyote. "I am going to a good hostel. I am going to have the most expensive dinner obtainable on Phoenix-One. I am going to buy six bottles of the best beer this place has got. And then I am going to sleep for twelve hours. And *then* I am going to Galoralon."

"How long," asked the robot primly, "will this program take, Citizen?"

"Have the flyer fueled and ready to go at ten o'clock tomorrow morning," Coyote said. "After breakfast. A *leisurely* breakfast."

"Very good, Citizen Student."

Very good, Citizen Student? And just who had paid for the fancy programming that enabled this machine to recognize him as a Student? Waste! Conspicuous waste! Coyote restrained the impulse to kick its pedestal, and contented himself with patting it on its little pointed head.

*   *   *

WELCOME TO GALORALON! said the sign.

In letters sixteen feet tall. They were not, unfortunately, either tall enough or thick enough to hide the view, which went on forever. Flat. Flat as Kanzas, as the saying went. Everything was pale green as far as the eye could see, and that was incredibly far. Sinkholes and potholes and an occasional drainage ditch. Pale green thickets and pale green trees, from which dangled pale green vines and pale green snakes. Over pale green mud, through which bubbles rose from time to time with a soft pop. And none of this green was the pale green of tender April buds, either; it was a shade more properly associated with medical textbooks.

Pheew.

Coyote landed the flyer on the pad, and congratulated himself when it didn't sink into the slime. They did not call Galoralon "The Swamp Planet" as a joke; they had excellent reasons. It was almost all swamp, and where it was not swamp it was bare tundra with a kind of scruffy gray grass. It was the kind of place that matched a really bad hangover perfectly. It had four continents, each more revolting than the last, and a total population of just over eleven million miserable people. Most of them lived on the continent of Krausse, where a city of sorts had been built on tundra chunks and government-issue floaters, along with a small landing-port. The city, predictably, was called Krausseburg, and its entire complement of flat, boxy structures stretched away before Coyote's eyes, perched on stilts above the ground, for when the swamps rose in the fall.

They came out to meet him, which he had not expected, and there were five of them, also unexpected.

"Citizen Coyote Jones?" said one of them.

"Right," said Coyote, and before he could get out another word—to point out, for example, that his name had *three* syllables, not two—they had a restraining net over him.

"You are under arrest," said the short fat one who appeared to be in charge. Another one reached into the flyer and pulled out the satchel and the guitar case and took off with them in the general direction of the port building. The others poked him rudely in the back and shoulders.

"Move it!" they said in chorus.

Coyote set his feet firmly and stood as still as possible, since the net would tighten automatically in response to anything remotely like a struggle.

"Just a minute," he said. "You've made a mistake. I realize I'm somewhat . . . unusually . . . dressed, Citizens, but I am in fact a federal agent on a very important mission, and if you'll just let me get to my credentials—"

"Shut up, Citizen Jones," said the fat one. "We are quite aware that you are a TGIS man. You make a lousy Student."

"In that case—"

The man's voice rose to a shrill and ear-puncturing scream. "And we are sick and *tired* of the continual efforts of the Tri-Galactic Intelligence Service to interfere in the internal affairs of Galoralon!"

"But—"

"And we are *aware*, Citizen, that you come to stir up revolution among our nomadic peoples and cause them to rise against our benevolent government, which—the Light knows— has nothing but their best interests at heart."

"I just—"

The man shook a thick fist in Coyote's face and jerked at the restraining net until it tightened enough to satisfy him.

"Enough!" he screamed. "We have the evidence, Citizen Jones! We know what we are talking about! Enough!"

He snapped his fingers, there was a flicker of cold at the back of Coyote's neck, and everything went . . . in the best secret-agent tradition . . . black. Everything Went Black.

When he came to, he was in a small room, sitting in a chair facing the five of them. Plus a woman in the uniform of a Federation Outpost Marshal. His tattoos were all in place, the restraining net was gone, and his mouth tasted of swamp gas.

"Citizen Jones," asked the Marshal courteously, "are you sufficiently awake to view the evidence against you?"

"I need some air," said Coyote crossly, "You apparently include injections of swampwater in your hospitable welcomes to this garden planet."

The Marshal nodded to the others. "We'll go out on the balcony," she said. "It's logical that he should feel the need of fresh air. Citizen Jones, do not try to escape, or we will be forced to give you another of those . . . swampwater . . . injections.''

"I wouldn't think of it, Citizen Marshal," Coyote cooed. "Besides, I wouldn't want to miss the view from your balcony. What is it, waterfalls?''

It was of course tundra, bordered by swamp, and a long line of square lumpy dwellings and buildings strung out along a pale green road, but they said nothing. No doubt if you were a Citizen of Galoralon, you quickly became immune to slurs on your homeworld's physical beauty.

"Please sit down, Citizen Jones," said the Marshal. "And you, Citizens.''

"May I speak, Citizen Marshal?'' demanded Coyote.

"Offworld dog, be silent!'' bellowed one of the men, and Coyote looked at him in genuine astonishment. Even in the antiquated threedies he'd seen while waiting in the landing pattern for Phoenix-One, there'd been nobody with the nerve to say "offworld dog.''

"It is you who will be silent, Citizen Hupp," said the Marshal crisply. "The offworld Citizen may speak.''

"I would like to know precisely what I'm charged with,'' said Coyote, "and on what ridiculous basis, and then I would like to get on with my mission.''

"The charge,'' she told him, "is inciting revolution. The basis is anything but ridiculous.''

She pointed to the man on her right, saying, "Evidence, please, Gordeyn," and the man slapped a flat packet smartly into her outstretched hand.

"This was found hidden inside the lining of your guitar case, Citizen Jones,'' said the Marshal. "Examine it, please.''

He did, shaking the contents out and shuffling through them rapidly. It was an appallingly amateur array of junk. The kind of thing you might get if you sent off for a ''Junior Secret Agent Kit.'' There was a microcassette labeled ''Nomads of the Swamps, Arise Against Your Tormentors!'' There was a cheap machine for making duplicates of the cassette. There were negatives of some revolutionary posters. There was a bad map of the swamps of Krausse, there was a detailed—

and pitiful—scenario laying out his alleged plans for foment-
ing this revolution. And there was a packet of lapel buttons
reading WHIP INIQUITY NOW.

Coyote stared mournfully at this assortment of trivia, and
then at the Marshal, who informed him that the case seemed
swamp-gas tight to her.

"At this very moment," said Citizen Hupp ominously
from his Marshal's side, tugging at the lapels of his bolero,
"the nomadic peoples of Krausse, some half a million strong,
are gathering in the swamps that encircle this beautiful city."
He waved his arms in an enormous circle. "At this very
moment," he repeated, "they come by the hundreds of thousands to celebrate their traditional Festival of the Seventh
Year. And if we had not learned of the wicked, vicious,
despicable plot against us, if we had not, I say, come to find
out, by the merest, the most fortuitous chance, that—"

Coyote waited for an open space to come along in the
man's tirade, and then he asked casually, "Is an offworld
woman named Drussa Silver leading this horde of nomads, by
any chance?"

Hupp's completely blank expression provided him the answer he had expected, and the rest of the man's ravings were
drowned out by the pounding of blood in his ears.

In the first place, he'd been had. Nobody but good old
Dean Shandalynne O'Halloran, his friendly neighborhood
briefer, with her abstracts and her tattoos and her expert
advice about how simple everything would be, had sufficient
power to pull off a thing like this. He had been royally,
imperially, pontifically *had*. And now he was supposed to be
dragged off to jail, where he would sit for months, if he was
lucky, and years, if he wasn't. While the TGIS tried to
negotiate diplomatically for his release, all the while denying
that they had ever heard of him. He was supposed to be pretty
helpless, of course, so far as the Dean was concerned, since
she had no knowledge of the particular skill that had gotten
him stuck in TGIS to begin with.

In the second place, somebody had taken a laser, or a
knife—godforbidandfend, a knife! or who knew? on this
place, perhaps a pointed stick?—and had torn up his guitar

case. Coyote didn't like that. That guitar case was a museum piece, an irreplaceable antique lavender-plush-lined museum piece, and while he didn't mind people looking at it, or touching it, the thought of somebody slashing into its heart and hiding things there made his beard stand on end. The idea of somebody slashing in there to get the things back *out* was unbearable.

And in the third—and most important—place, his pride had been done an injury from which he was not sure it would recover. The *idea* that he, Coyote Jones, strongest projective telepath in three galaxies, a man able to control rioting thousands at a distance of damn near a mile, had come here to start a revolution with *lapel buttons!* Why not say he'd planned next to fly out over the swamps dropping paper leaflets out the window in little plastic envelopes? It was past bearing, and he didn't intend to bear it.

If he had not been so totally enraged, he might have thought twice about what he did next. If he had not just happened to know that the administration of Galoralon was indeed corrupt and wicked and soundly deserving of overthrow, he might have hesitated. If he had not been someone who firmly believed that not all good things must be totally devoid of laughter, he might have waited a bit. But none of those factors happened to be relevant here, and he didn't consider them for a second.

Instead, he leaned forward a little, took a deep breath, and projected. At full strength, in all directions, and with the greatest of joy:

PEOPLE OF GALORALON!

PEOPLE OF THE PALE GREEN SWAMPS!

PEOPLE OF THE TWINING SNAKES, LIMPID AMONG THE TREES!

FLOWER OF THE GALORALON OUTLANDS, OH BEARERS OF DESTINY, I CALL ON YOU!

THE TIME HAS COME . . . . TO THROW OFF THE CHAINS OF OPPRESSION!

THE TIME HAS COME . . . . . TO RISE AGAINST YOUR WICKED MASTERS!

HOW LONG, O PEOPLE OF THE MIRE AND OF THE SCENTED MIASMAS, WILL YOU TOLERATE THE BRUTAL FOOLS WHOSE HEELS ARE SET UPON YOUR PROSTRATE THROATS? HOW LONG, HOW LONG? ARE YOU HUMAN BEINGS, OR ARE YOU SLIME MOLDS?

COME DOWN INTO THE CITY, O NOBLE PEOPLE OF THE SWAMPS, AND CUT DOWN THE DOGS WHO DARE TO SIT IN THE SEATS OF GOVERNMENT THAT ARE RIGHTFULLY YOURS AND YOURS ALONE! HAVE NO FEAR, THERE ARE ONLY A HANDFUL OF THEM!

O PEOPLE OF GALORALON, O NOBLE NOMAD PEOPLE, ARISE! THE PRESIDENT IS A FOOL AND A WEAKLING, DRUNK HALF THE TIME AND DRUGGED THE REST, HE CANNOT STAND AGAINST YOU! HIS MEN ARE FOOLS AND WEAKLINGS LIKE HIM, COME FORWARD AND CUT THEM DOWN!

A SWAMP-NOMAD SHALL SIT IN THE PRESIDENT'S CHAIR AND WRITE AT THE PRESIDENT'S DESK! HURRAH!

A SWAMP-NOMAD SHALL WEAR THE ELEVEN-POINTED STAR OF JUSTICE AND THE GRAY RIBBON OF IMPERIAL PURITY! HURRAH!

O NOBLE PEOPLE, O NOBLE NOMADS, HARKEN TO ME! ETC., ETC.

He had a wonderful time. The longer it went on, the more he warmed to it, and by the time the first wave of them came over the balcony rail, he was really enjoying himself. After all, he'd put down more riots than he could count, but this was the first one he'd ever *started*.

He went up on the roof to avoid the crush, and stuck around long enough, projecting encouraging words and sustaining songs, to see the President being carried away trussed up in vines like a pig, and a pallid greenish nomad sitting behind the Presidential desk with a stylus in his hand, drafting a State-of-the-Planet Message. Then he headed for the port and his flyer, pausing only long enough to snatch up his satchel and his guitar. He left his mutilated guitar case behind.

The roar from the city behind him as he took off was a source of great satisfaction to him. He wished only that the Dean could hear it, too.

Chapter Four

The definition of the word "lie" has nothing to do with the word "truth," which is not its antonym. A sequence of words can be defined as a "truth" or as a "lie" only in terms of the degree to which it achieves the purpose for which it was intended.

—Manual of the Tri-Galactic
Intelligence Service, p. 16

He was a man of some importance. He was called The Fish, for his coldness of blood. Chief of the Tri-Galactic Intelligence Service most of his adult life, he had at his disposal at all times three hundred fifty hand-picked operatives with very special skills, and a maintenance staff of two hundred live persons, seven thousand Fedrobots, and three Central-computer terminals.

He could order people killed. He could manipulate the internal affairs of entire countries. He could make the top officials of continents tremble, by a chance word casually dropped. It was therefore interesting that the arrival of a message saying that Citizen Dean Shandalynne O'Halloran of Multiversity Two was waiting to see him made him want to hide under his desk.

He had just decided to instruct the Amanuensis Mark IV to advise the Dean that he was out, when the din coming from his outer office reached a frightening intensity and the panicbutton glowed red on his comset's office panel, throwing open the communicator to let him hear just what was really going on.

"Sir," said the voice of the Amanuensis, "the Citizen Dean wishes to advise—"

"The Citizen Dean wishes to advise bedamned!" The Dean's bellow cut over the computer like a buzz saw whipping through standing grain. "Either you see me, *now,* Alvin Wythllewyn, or—"

The Fish did not wait to see what the alternative to his compliance was going to be, although he felt a certain natural curiosity. At the sound of his name, which had not been uttered or written inside or outside TGIS in at least twenty-five years, he went stark white and slammed the communicator stud, shouting, "Send her in! Send her in!"

The door slid soundlessly open, and the Dean came in, smiling. "I thought that would do it," she said.

"Unfair!" said The Fish bitterly. "Really unfair, Citizen Dean."

"You should be flattered," she pointed out, "that I *remember* your name. It's been better than thirty years since you were a Student of mine, Alvin, and I've seen many many hundreds come and go in that time."

The Fish glared at her and motioned to the antique chair that faced his desk.

"Do please sit down, Citizen Dean," he said. "Please."

Shandalynne O'Halloran looked the chair over from the back, and then she walked around it and looked at it from several other angles, and her mouth puckered, along with her eyebrows.

"That chair," she said, "was carefully chosen to make whoever sits in it miserable. The back is too low, so that you can't lean back without it striking you right over the kidneys. The arms slant up, so you can't rest your elbows without making your shoulders ache. The seat slants down so that you get cramps in your legs. That's not a chair, Alvin, it's a torture instrument. Is it electric, too?"

"That chair cost fifty-seven decacredits," said The Fish. "It deserves respect for its age and its long and faithful service, however odd it may be otherwise."

The Dean chuckled. "You always were a sneaky man, Alvin," she said. "and I see that you have not changed your ways. Fortunately for me, however, I deal with sneaky little men all the time."

She opened the pocket of her tunic, took out a small flat packet of dark blue plastic, pulled a tiny silver plug in one corner, watched serenely through the soft hissing of air, and then sat in the resulting chair. Even for an inflatable, it was elegant. And very comfortable.

"Now then," she said. "I want to talk to you."

The Fish waited, and she leaned back in her chair and smiled at him, and *she* waited.

"What about?"

"About one Citizen Coyote Jones," she said promptly, "who I hear is one of your TGIS men, and who appeared on my doorstep a few days back sporting a conservative loincloth, a wooden guitar, a bright red beard, and a veritable cornucopia of official directives which can easily be summarized as follows: Give This Man Anything He Wants and Don't Ask Questions."

"Hmmmmmmm," said The Fish.

"It took me some time to find out who his chief was," she said.

"I'm glad to hear that."

"It didn't take me *very* long."

"Hmmmmmm," said the Fish again, and flashed his beautiful white teeth.

"Now," the Dean went on, "when this personage arrived to see me, I was informed that he was to be assisted in masquerading as a Student, on his way to the planet Freeway to do a dissertation comparing the effects of the Maklunite religion on various cultures with the effects of the Shavvy religion on the culture of Freeway specifically. I was not told why, but was given to understand that the fate of the universe et cetera, et cetera, hung upon the success of his mission."

"That," observed The Fish, "was something of an overstatement."

"Oh?"

"Well . . . it was important, but we will not actually crumble into the void if he fails."

"If he fails to what?"

"I beg your pardon?"

"I said, if he fails to *what?* What precisely is this poor crippled gentleman supposed to be doing?"

"Crippled?" The Fish registered, for once, genuine amazement.

"Certainly. Your man's mind-deaf—didn't you even know that?"

"Crippled . . ." The Fish thought of a time when Coyote Jones had faced an advancing group of three hundred and ten tanks, each manned by a suicide squad of Haxxite warriors, each armed with a nuclear warhead, and had needed only thirteen seconds to convince the whole bunch to ride docilely around in circles until their fuel was exhausted. And then he thought of the concept of Coyote as a cripple, and snickered softly.

"Alvin, are you listening to me or not?"

The Fish jumped slightly, and leaned toward her attentively.

"Of course," he said.

"I have been asking you, Alvin, what the man's mission is. A simple question."

"And one that you surely understand I cannot answer."

"Nonsense."

"My dear Citizen Dean," protested The Fish, "you can't expect me to divulge to you a secret mission of extreme importance and delicacy with possible intergalactic repercussions that—"

"Then," snapped the Dean, "you can expect *me* to divulge to the press that I have been pressured into taking part in a fraud, passing off a TGIS man as a Student of Religion, and that my own important and delicate conscience will no longer allow me to remain silent about it all. In fact, at this very moment I feel the pressure to confess creeping over me, Alvin . . . irresistibly."

"Would you really do that?" demanded The Fish, pained. "Have you no sense of the propriety of things?"

She faced him stonily, tapping the edge of his desk with one finger.

"I'll have you assassinated," he ventured. "A little drug in the night, as you sit studying by your window. . . . The headlines will read 'Mysterious Disappearance of Venerable Dean Baffles Authorities.' "

The Dean snorted. "You couldn't get away with it," she said contemptuously. "Assassinate all the heads of government you like, but you try assassinating *me*, Alvin, and it will be *your* disappearance that baffles the authorities."

The Fish thought it over, and decided she was probably right.

"The publicity would be terrible," he mused.

"Alvin!" she said. "Talk, and stop all this silly posturing!"

People did not talk to The Fish like that, and she knew it, but he had no opportunity to say any of the things that immediately occurred to him, because she was way ahead of him.

"Ah, Citizen Director," she sighed, all charm and feathers, "you must forgive the eccentricities of an aged academician, unaccustomed to dealing with the outside world."

"You would tell on us, though," said The Fish.

"In an instant."

The Fish made a mental note that future operations must not on any account involve Multiversity Deans, made a second note that whoever had suggested it this time was to be fired, and prepared to negotiate.

"May I ask what it is that has alarmed you so?" he asked, for beginners. "Did Citizen Jones insult you? Threaten you? Did you find his mission offensive to some personal principle?"

"Jones was . . . diverted . . . briefly from his mission," said the Dean, "and landed on Galoralon."

The Fish looked very surprised. "Really," he said.

"And," the Dean went on, "by some astonishing coincidence, only an hour after his landing, there was a revolution on Galoralon. Those who managed to flee report that the people of the swamps just spontaneously, with no warning at all, rose up and took over the government. 'As if inspired by a force outside themselves' was the phrase used in the threedies, as I recall.''

"And?''

"And I don't believe in coincidences.''

"Nor do I,'' said The Fish significantly.

"Which means?''

"The diversion,'' he said. "The so-called diversion.''

"Well.''

"Well, what?''

"I am quite willing to admit that I had something to do with that.''

"That does not surprise me.''

"And I am also quite willing to admit that it didn't work. Your TGIS man was *supposed* to be at this moment languishing in a Galoralon jail, inhaling the swamp gases and counting off the days on his cell wall with little drops of his blood, obtained by biting his thumb each morning.''

"A certain element of delay, eh, Citizen Dean?''

"Precisely.''

"And this 'cripple' managed to escape unscathed?''

"Indeed he did,'' said the Dean bitterly. "Right on to Freeway, with not even a full day lost.''

"Hmmmmm.''

"It comes of doing things without proper motivation,'' said the Dean.

"Explain, please?''

"It comes, Alvin, of having delayed your Citizen Jones—or rather, having tried to do so—without knowing exactly why I was taking that step. A certain feeling of distrust . . . a nagging concern that he was going to cause trouble and I wasn't sure what *sort* of trouble . . . these are not proper motivations.''

The Fish looked at her sternly, and pronounced, "*Nothing* is a proper motivation for a Multiversity Dean to interfere in the activities of a federal bureau.''

"BEM-dung,'' said the Dean. "For everything, no matter what, there can always be—logically speaking—a proper motivation.''

"Citizen," snapped The Fish, "we are not dealing in logic here, we are dealing in reality!"

"Then," said the Dean, leaning toward him, "let me set you the reality as if it *were* a logical problem. *Given:* one apparently crippled semi-idiot, tootling about the Galaxies on a secret mission. *Given:* one pleasant and inoffensive little religious movement, on a Novice Planet called Freeway, somehow involved in this mission. *Given:* one 'spontaneous' revolution, somehow involved with the activities of the crippled semi-idiot. *Given:* a universe full of *real* problems to be solved, *real* revolutions to be fought, *real* missions to send people on! And *needed,* my friend, some mechanism for deriving sensible conclusions . . . or just *sense* . . . from this array of givens. Now just what the *devil* is going on?"

She leaned back in the chair again and looked him straight in the eye. "I warn you, Alvin," she said softly, "I mean to know."

"Ah well," said The Fish, sighing enormously. "I'll tell you, then."

"I'm waiting."

"Simple enough," said The Fish. "We have sent Coyote Jones out to Freeway—using the Student cover, supplied with your excellent help, thank you very much—to find Drussa Silver, charge her with violating Galactic Regulation Seventeen, and to bring her back here for trial. At the request of the government of Freeway, I might add."

"The government of Freeway is primitive," said the Dean. "And corrupt."

"It is nonetheless entitled to ask for help from Mars-Central, like any other member of the Federation."

"The people of Freeway are oppressed and degraded by this government, which has them locked into a feudal system reminiscent of the Middle Ages of Old Earth!"

"There is a mechanism available to them," said The Fish calmly. "They need only file a Complaint Of Oppression with the Tri-Galactic Council, and they have not done so."

"They are not even *aware* that they are oppressed!"

"Then," said The Fish, "they are not yet ready to be mucked about with by the investigatory panels and jurists and legislators of the Tri-Galactic Federation. Freeway is still on Novice Planet status. Its government is still playing at sovereignty and ordering everyone to stay out of its territory—standard Novice behavior. They will need another ten, perhaps twenty years, before it is possible to bring them fully into the Federation without imposing severe shock upon their culture."

The Dean's eyes narrowed.

"A policy of benign noninterference, eh?"

"That is customary."

"Then what right have you to 'muck about' in their religious affairs?" thundered the Dean. "Galactic Regulation Seventeen, for the Light's sake! Using religion to defraud the *people?* Can you find me a Novice Planet where that regulation is *not* being violated?"

The Fish spread his hands in a gesture of helplessness.

"I repeat," he said, "we were asked to interfere by the government of the planet, which claims that this female charlatan is wreaking havoc with her mumbo-jumbo."

"What mumbo-jumbo?"

"She is," said The Fish patiently, "possessed of unusual psibilities, we are told, and is able to produce mass hallucinations of high quality and great ingenuity. She has convinced a high proportion of the masses on Freeway that she is capable of a wide assortment of miracles, and this conviction is causing massive defections of people of Freeway from their establishment culture. The government feels it can't be allowed to go on, and has asked for help—which is perfectly within their rights."

There was a long silence, while the Dean looked at him, and then she said, "What makes you so sure she is a fake, Alvin?"

The Fish raised his eyebrows. "Oh, come now," he scoffed, "do you believe that people can walk on the ocean barefooted? Fly through the air under their own power? Bring down showers of roses and lilies from heaven? Start and stop storms? Make it snow in summer heat? Make rocks sing—in four-part *harmony?*"

"You obviously don't."

"No, I certainly do not, and neither does any other thinking person. Some of the tricks are easily explained . . . some sort of gravity-repellent substance on the feet for the traipsing about on the ocean, a concealed mechanical device for the seeming independent flight . . . the others are clearly telepathic projections.''

''And Citizen Jones is to do what?''

The Fish smiled. ''Ah,'' he said with great satisfaction, ''Citizen Jones is *immune* to her little tricks! As you noticed, he is mind-deaf, and he will have no difficulty exposing Drussa Silver for the fraud she is. Others will see showers of roses; Coyote Jones won't. It is that simple.''

The Dean stared down at her hands and said nothing, and The Fish, who remembered her very well, considered this an alarming sign. Any moment, for example, she might well ask him why on earth, if Coyote Jones was suited for this mission only because he was mind-deaf, he was a TGIS man at all. Or she might remember the curious juxtaposition of Coyote and the Galoralon revolution, and demand an explanation for that. At which point he would have to lie, and lie convincingly enough to fool Shandalynne O'Halloran. It was not a prospect that appealed to him. It struck him as a good moment to send for liquid refreshments, and he did that, including the code words that meant do-it-faster-than-it-is-possible-to-do-it-or-else.

When the Dean did speak, however, she did not raise the questions he had anticipated. Instead, she asked a question that made him wonder if she was getting old.

''What,'' she asked him, ''if Drussa Silver is *not* a fraud?''

That was an easy one. Or a trick. He was not sure which.

''Impossible,'' he said.

''Why?''

''Either she's a fraud or she's divine,'' he said flatly. ''An avatar, an incarnation of the divine in human form . . . and if she's that, I'm Michaelmouse.''

''Why again?''

''In the first place, all avatars are male,'' said The Fish, pouring the drinks. ''Please note: Christ, Buddha, Mohammed, Lao-Tzu, et cetera, et cetera, et cetera. Not a female in the lot. In the second place, divine beings belong in the same spacebucket as the Easter Bunny, the Santa Claus, the Tooth Fairy, the Helga Dik, and the supposed benefits of taxation. You know that. I know that. *Despite* the fact that you are trained in a curious discipline called Religious Science, you know that."

"Alvin—"

"*And*," he charged on, "*if* she is genuine—which is impossible, but I'm a tolerant man, and willing to humor an aged and eccentric academician—if, I say, she is genuine, there'll be no problem. Coyote will bring her back, she'll stand trial, she'll be acquitted, we'll send her home first-class by government rocket—unless, of course, she prefers to fly home under her own power through space, breathing the perfume of roses and lilies—and that will be that. End of episode."

"I see," said the Dean.

"You see!" The Fish laughed. "All that explanation, dragged out of me by blackmail—oh yes, it *was*, Citizen Dean, shameless blackmail—and all you can say is 'I see.' Aren't you satisfied?"

The Dean leaned back, her hands in an attitude of prayer, and tapped her fingertips together lightly, thinking.

"Almost," she said. "Almost."

Ahah! thought The Fish. The Dean had never been one to lose track of the thread of an argument.

"You have been most cooperative," she said.

"Thank you."

"However . . ."

"Yes?"

"I would still like to know *precisely* the connection between your man and the revolution on Galoralon. Three-thousand-some-odd years those swamp nomads have fiddled along without the slightest sign of political feeling, and then suddenly, on the one day, at the one hour, when Coyote Jones lands, *wham! bang-o!* A total overturn of the government!"

"And I," said The Fish pleasantly, "would like to know *precisely* how you managed to—divert, as you put it—an agent of this bureau, land him on a swamp planet, and damned near get him arrested and thrown in jail to languish for months as an embarrassment to the Federation and the TGIS.''

"Touché," said the Dean.

"I think so."

Shandalynne O'Halloran stood up and smoothed her rumpled tunic. She tapped the control on her inflatable chair, watched as it shrank docilely to nothing, folded it up neatly, and put it back in her pocket.

"Delighted to have had a chance for this little visit," she said heartily. "You must come and see *me* some time."

"On Harvard?" said The Fish with horror.

"Certainly, on Harvard. That is where I am to be found."

"I do not travel," said The Fish stiffly. "I do not have time."

"And," said the Dean, "you suffer from space-sickness."

"How," he asked disgustedly, "can you possibly remember *that?*"

She gave him a significant look and one last smile.

"Deans," she said as she turned to leave, "remember *everything.*"

The door closed soundlessly behind her, and he sat there feeling that he'd gotten off reasonably well, since she had somehow not asked the one *really* awkward question. He only hoped that that did not mean she already knew its answer.

II

Shandalynne O'Halloran knew that she was not being very polite. Certainly she was not fulfilling her obligations to this Advanced Student whose turn it was to spend the evening in her company. Since each Student got only one such turn, it was unbecoming of her not to rise to the occasion and Be A Dean, concerned only with the problems of this Student.

Especially this Student, who was one of her favorites. Ai-Myn, she was called, and she was an Angel. Not really, of course; technically speaking she was a Hequelian, a Citizen of the third of the Extreme Moons. But it was not possible to look at the Hequelians, note the height and slender elegance, the extraordinary beauty of their faces, the soft clusters of short golden curls that framed those faces, and not understand why the Terran space captain who first encountered them had said immediately—"Angels!" The vestigial white-feathered wings had done nothing to discourage the perpetuation of the nickname.

"You are thoughtful tonight, Citizen Dean," said the Student. "Your mind is . . . devoted to a question."

"No," said the Dean. "Not quite. My mind is devoted, rather, to a puzzle. Perhaps two puzzles."

"And you expect to find the answer in there?"

The Student pointed at the microfiche the Dean had been holding when she came in and had been turning round and round in her hands ever since.

The Dean set the thing down, guiltily. This really was not fair to the Student, to come to her for this one evening in which, according to tradition, she was to have the opportunity to take up her own problems with the Dean, and find that Dean obsessed with something else.

"It is *Woman Transcendent*," said the Dean. "I had a feeling, somehow, that when I read it . . . long ago . . . there was something in there that applied to the—the puzzles. But I've been reading it over for hours, and whatever it was that I thought was there, I can't find it."

"Can I help, perhaps?" asked Ai-Myn. "Sometimes another person can find the missing piece because she has not been looking for it with such intensity."

The Dean nodded. "Quite right," she said. "And perhaps you can, if you are willing to do something very trivial."

"Anything at all," said Ai-Myn. "Only ask me."

"Then," said the Dean, "do this for me. *Woman Transcendent* is a basic text. On every elementary reading list. It is not something with which a Student at your level any longer spends much time. But could you state for me, just to give my own thinking the benefit of yours, the basic principles which Ann Geheygan established with the book?"

This was a very superior Student. She did not hesitate for a moment.

"First principle:" she said, "that women achieve with ease that state of transcendence which men are able to attain only through great effort. Geheygan was, I believe, the first to name this state *surpassment*."

"Correct," said the Dean. "Continue, please."

"Second principle: in those times of prehistory when the greater physical strength of the male gave him a certain advantage, he noted this female talent for the transcendent state and recognized it as a great danger to patriarchal society.

"Third principle: as a way of protecting the patriarchy against this danger, men took it upon themselves to pervert the natural female religious talent, using the technique of convincing the female that what she *really* had was a talent not for surpassment but for submission. This perversion was maintained by the patriarchal religions down through the ages.

"Fourth principle:" said the Student, and she chuckled softly, "since these first three basics had been thoroughly suppressed by the male, to such an extent that most men had truly forgotten them, it was necessary for Geheygan to bring the facts to light and put an end to the ancient perversion."

"Well put," said the Dean with great satisfaction. It was a necessary skill for any Student—summarizing large amounts of information into a few well-constructed statements—but very few did it so well as this one. Especially on such short notice.

"Have I left anything out?" asked the Student hesitantly.

"Do you think so?"

"Well . . . Geheygan established that many of the so-called theological problems were only problems of linguistics . . . but that was not original with her. . . . No. I can think of nothing else. Have I helped you with your puzzles, Citizen Dean?"

"No," said the Dean, trying to hide the frustration in her voice, but sure she was doing it badly. "And I cannot understand it, Ai-Myn. I *know* that somewhere in this book— somewhere in the theological system of Ann Geheygan—is the clue. I remember, I remember in that maddening, maddening way, where it is right on the tip of one's mind. . . .Oh, Ai-Myn . . . let's drop this and speak of the things you have come to me to talk about. Come, we'll put my so-called puzzles aside, along with my memory, which is obviously failing me.''

''May I make just one suggestion?''

''Of course,'' said the Dean. ''Have you thought of something else?''

''Perhaps what you remember is not in *Woman Transcendent*. Perhaps it is, instead, in Geheygan's earlier work.''

The Dean's eyes widened.

''Her earlier work?'' she said slowly. ''I had forgotten—if I ever knew—that there was earlier work by Geheygan.''

''Assuredly. There was a very short book, written when she was quite young. The book for which she was discharged from her teaching position. It was called *A Handbook for the Great De-Fathering Festival*.''

''Of course!'' The Dean smacked her forehead with her open palm. ''My memory *is* failing, you see. I had forgotten all about the *Handbook*.''

''Perhaps,'' said the Student gently, ''what you seek is there.''

The Dean grinned and took the Student into her ample arms.

''Probably,'' she said. ''Probably so. And now we will talk only of you.''

Chapter Five

I can hear what you are stinking,
I can smell what you are thinking!

If your mother catches you
She'll turn your brains to
      Stinky-Stew!

—obscene children's jingle,
from the planet Freeway

Coyote brought the flyer down out of the dawn sky and entered the territorial space surrounding Freeway. The sky all about him was thick with clouds, pale fluff shot disneyly with rose, the planet lay below him wrapped in its emerald forests and trailing fogs, for all the world like the northwestern coasts of North America on Old Earth, and he was slightly giddy with it all. As he was constantly being told, his greatest fault after his obsessive curiosity was the romanticism that he could not seem to outgrow, and he was a real sucker for trailing fogs and rosy clouds. Not to mention emerald forests of giant trees that they might call nishia-bella all they wanted to, but that looked like super-redwoods to *him*. Ah, glory. Hallelujah. He longed for an appropriate word of sufficient power and majesty, but it escaped him.

He pressed the overhead communication bar and requested permission to land, and the answering voice ripped right through the mists and the clouds and slapped him back into a state of empirical pragmatism.

"Landing on Freeway is forbidden," it said. "We have no tourist industry. Please move on, with our official regrets."

"I have a landing pass," Coyote protested. "Don't you think you ought to ask first? Before you burden people with your official regrets?"

There was a brief silence, and then the voice spoke again.

"Cite your pass numbers, please, and your priority."

"Seven, eight eleven, four. Priority Two."

"Priority Two? Nobody gets Priority Two for Freeway."

"Priority Two."

"Priority Two . . ." fussed the voice. It was turning into a kind of chant for two voices, and Coyote was tired of it.

"Right!" he snapped. "Let's get on with it."

"One moment, please, Citizen Offworlder, while this is verified . . . . Yes. There we are. Landing Pass number seven, eight eleven, four. Priority Two, issued to Citizen Coyote Jones—" The voice stopped abruptly, and then went on. "Student," it said carefully, with strong dubious overtones.

"Right again."

The voice cleared its throat.

"Permission granted to land," it said. "Stand by for Hook."

Coyote had only time to bellow a protest before the Hook had him and he was literally snatched out of the sky and deposited, stomach in throat, on a neat gray landingpad.

"Significant BEM-dung!" he shouted, slamming the communication bar with his fist, "what's the matter with you people? Didn't you ever hear of warnings? Not to mention, didn't you ever hear of civilization?"

"Travel to Freeway," said the voice crisply, "is strongly discouraged. We find that having Hook facilities as the only possible method of landing constitutes a powerful discouragement, particularly to sporty types in sky-yachts."

Coyote sat there, taking deep breaths, and trying to regain at least a semblance of equilibrium before he had to face whoever was attached to the voice. The Fish had not told him about the Hook landing, although he had undoubtedly known about it and was just as undoubtedly sitting in his office on Mars-Central at this very moment chuckling and snickering at the little surprise he had reserved for his trusty agent. Just one of the little side-benefits of TGIS service. May his eyebrows decay and sink into his head . . .

"Citizen Jones?"

"Yes?"

"Will you please proceed to the port for processing. Do not move your belongings; they will be scanned and brought to you in approximately three minutes. Terminate."

Terminate. Coyote sat there muttering to himself. I'd terminate you personally if I was only passing through. I'd terminate you into an unshakable conviction that you were a hybrid Maltokian lizard, for example, and feed you worms, photographing all the while for later replay.

However, he had not been sent here to vent his frustrations on petty rocketport officials.

He inventoried his internal organs and satisfied himself that they had all recovered from the state of numbed shock induced by the Hook snatch and were back in their normal positions in his interior, and then he opened the flyer door and sauntered along the landing ramp to a bubbleport so grimly like every other bubbleport that he was sure it was intended to be yet another "discouragement" to the unwary traveler. Unfortunately for those planning the effects, however, it was unlikely to even be noticed. You could have set the caldrons of Hell down in this port and they would have gone unnoticed. The little bubble's standard-issue gray-and-green-splotch surface was no match for the majesty of the towering trees that surrounded it in every direction, and no arriving tourist would have looked at it twice.

He had been prepared somewhat, in an intellectual sense, for the nishia-bella trees, having seen the scrap of threedy film on Mars-Central. But seen up close they nonetheless took his breath away. The closest one had a trunk that would have had to be at least eighty feet in diameter, and it was one of the middle-sized ones. The only way to see the top would be to lie flat on your back on the ground. Sunlight laced down through the tree crowns in ribbons and patches, emerald-colored ferns rose higher than his head, and the air smelled like dry wine and fresh-cut grass and leafmold, with a touch of something else he could not identify. He might never go home.

The door of the bubbleport stuck . . . more discouragements. He palmed it impatiently, which of course made it fly open as he leaned against it, catapulting him into the room bereft of all dignity. He was pleased to note, once he had recovered his balance, that there was nobody there but a blah-looking computer with a yellow light on top.

As he turned to look at it, the yellow light changed briefly to red, and the computer spoke.

"Welcome to Freeway, Citizen Jones," it said.

"Well!" said Coyote. "I never would have recognized *you* as a computer."

"In view of the violence you were undoubtedly contemplating upon my person, it is perhaps just as well that I am not made of flesh and blood," the machine observed. "Although I am an older model, and not completely impervious to a persistent attack."

"What makes you think I was contemplating violence?"

"I am programmed to assess voice quality, Citizen Jones, and I am very expensive."

"Top class, eh?"

"Correct. No trouble or expense was spared in my construction."

Coyote was considering a really smart-ass reply to this when the door of the bubbleport burst open again and a large, rangy man wearing an elaborate costume of green-and-white synthosilk came charging through.

"Agamen Horta Cady, Noble of Castle Olyon, Sector Five," said the computer. "Citizen Cady, Citizen Coyote Jones, Student of Multiversity Two, Asteroid Harvard, First Galaxy."

Cady glared fiercely at the computer.

"Have that door fixed," he said furiously. "There's no excuse for such ineptitude!"

"Contrary to programmed orders," said the computer. "I regret that I cannot comply."

"What kind of mechanized nonsense—"

The computer interrupted him smoothly.

"A primary element of assessment of all arrivals on Freeway is based upon remarks made by visitors entering that door," it said. "The effect is of course negligible on repeat visitors, who invariably walk around the bubble until they find the other entrance."

"Hmmmph," said the big man, and he frowned at the machine.

"Please change the subject," it said. "This conversation is counterproductive."

Cady shrugged and turned to Coyote, pressing his fists to his chest in the Freeway greeting-gesture.

"Welcome, Citizen Student," he said. "Have your belongings been processed?"

"Just outside the door," the computer put in. "All conveniently tagged and ready to be taken away."

Cady turned on the computer and bellowed at it in a manner and at a volume that almost made Coyote envious. "*Will* you terminate!" he shouted, and the light at the top of the computer subsided to yellow.

"Can one apologize for the manners of a machine?" the man asked Coyote. "If so, consider that I have done so."

"No problem," said Coyote. "I am accustomed to recalcitrant machines which delight in tormenting humans."

"Machines do not feel delight, Citizen," said Cady, "nor do they feel any other emotion."

"Precisely the statement made about plants," said Coyote with his most charming smile, "until very late in the twentieth century."

"Really?"

"I assure you that it is so."

"How quaint," said Agamen Cady.

Coyote manfully restrained himself from making the obvious retort and smiled politely at his host. He wondered which of them was the most extraordinary in appearance. There he himself stood in a dark blue loincloth with a white pinstripe, his chest abloom with curly red hair and tasteful pseudo-tattoos, his fingers heavy with rings, his ankles clanking with bracelets. And there stood Agamen Horta Cady in full green-and-white striped trousers, bound at the ankle with green ribbons, and a transparent white shirt with flowing sleeves and cuffs, open almost to the waist, a dashing gold sash knotted about his middle, and his head a mass of improbable golden curls topped by a slender gold circlet, a kind of coronet. Coyote decided that they were both in the worst possible taste, from an abstract aesthetic point of view, and that there was no choosing between them for abominableness.

He followed Cady out the door, gathered up his two small bags, and joined the man in a triangular two-seater flyer at the edge of the landing-field.

"Ready, Citizen?" asked Agamen Cady.

"Ready for what?"

"Takeoff, of course."

"Anything like your Hook landing?"

Cady chuckled and pressed a small silver button beside his foot. The little flyer rose smoothly into the air without a trace of sound or vibration, and headed off through the trees.

"You didn't enjoy the landing, then, Citizen?"

"I most emphatically did not."

"It discourages tourists," Cady said. "It's quite a lot rougher than it has to be . . . a few modifications."

"But what about the ordinary landing made by a Citizen of Freeway?" Coyote demanded. "Surely they are not put through that every time they land."

Cady shrugged his shoulders, saying, "We do not travel, Citizen Jones. A man who lives in Paradise prefers his own hearth."

Coyote saw no indication that their vehicle was being steered by Cady. There were no controls of any kind, except for the silver button on the floor of the flyer. Yet it avoided trees and buildings with ease, even where the branches of the nishia-bellas were festooned with intricate ramps, platforms, stairways, and bridges.

"Is it alive?" he asked.

"What?"

"This seemingly ominiscient creature we ride in."

"Oh . . . sorry, Citizen. We are computer-controlled from Castle Olyon, where we are headed now. There it is, Citizen, just ahead of us."

Coyote looked at the thing looming up through the trees, and rubbed his beard thoughtfully, not sure what verbal response was possible. He had seen such architectural nightmares before, in the microfiches used for courses in Old Earth Culture. It rose to a height that would have been impressive anywhere but among the nishia-bella trees, and it had a little bit of everything. Flying buttresses. Fenestrations. Crenellations. Moats. Lacy balconies flung across space. Towers with little winding exterior staircases. A real, honest-to-Grimm castle, out of a fairy tale.

"Four hundred and seventy-five rooms, Citizen Jones," said Agamen Cady, with an unmistakable note of pride that provided Coyote with the cue he needed.

"Magnificent," he said. "I've never seen anything like it."

They landed on a round dais on the roof of the central portion of the castle, as easily and silently as a leaf settling onto a lawn, and stepped out. There were no nishia-bella trees inside the castle walls, Coyote noticed, but branches from those outside extended to cover the whole in a canopy of green shot with flickering gold. Everywhere he looked, people were moving busily along the pathways set into the trees themselves, completely unconcerned at being a hundred feet above the ground without so much as a handrail.

"Magnificent," he said again, except that this time he meant it.

"Thank you, Citizen!" Agamen Cady beamed at him, and Coyote beamed back.

"Mmmm . . ."

"Yes, Citizen Jones?"

"Could you tell me what our plans are? That is, what happens next?"

The man rubbed his hands together and teetered back and forth on his feet, which Coyote could see were bursting out of the dainty silver slippers and undoubtedly hurt like the devil.

"First," he said, "we will give you an opportunity to freshen up—"

Coyote shook his head. "Not required."

"Excellent, excellent. Then we will go at once to the meeting scheduled for this morning."

"A meeting."

"Yes. With the Reverend Rabbi-Pastor Sarah Dorcas Elimalek, our highest religious official. You will enjoy her company, Citizen, she is a witty woman."

"And powerful?"

Cady looked at him blandly, and Coyote looked back, trying to ignore the fact that the tattoo on his right buttock itched abominably, until he was certain the man was not just the posturing, pompous dandy he appeared to be, and they both dropped the duel of eyes.

"Certainly she is powerful," Agamen Cady said smoothly. "She leads the Old Faith. There are millions of citizens subject to her under Church rule. Will you follow me now, please?"

Whatever Coyote had expected inside the castle, it was not what he found. All that gingerbread and stone lace, out of the mists of time and ancient myth, on the outside. And inside— like the inside of a spaceliner. Chrome ramps and pyroceramic antigravity tubes, suspensor lights that followed them as they walked along the corridors, not a sign of wood or cloth or of any nonsynthetic material anywhere. No furnishings, no art objects. The whole like a surgery, or a freezing-down unit. The fancy-dress costume Agamen Cady wore was like a mobile wart on the inside of the castle, and Coyote was too taken aback even to comment. Besides, it might not have been diplomatic to do so; who knew what mental and aesthetic gymnastics might not be required to condition a human being to accept this kind of inner/outer mismatch?

He kept still and followed Cady into a small room like the inside of an egg, bare and flawless and softly lit by some invisible source. Cady reached up and touched a pale green dot on the ceiling, which immediately glowed brightly.

"Table," he said, and a small conference table was extruded by the floor, so swiftly that Coyote barely had leisure to jump out of its way. The man from Castle Olyon was showing off.

"Three chairs," he said, and they appeared.

"Drinks," he said, and a niche opened in the far well, revealing a tray of bottles and glasses which proceeded under its own power over to the table, settling onto an attractor stud with a soft click.

Coyote would have liked to sit down; he had had about as many silly surprises as he could tolerate for one day. (Not that he had never seen a computer interior like this before. He had seen the sort that you only had to *think* at to get what you wanted, and many that would make all this look primitive. Nevertheless, never had he seen an inside so at odds with its outside.) But his host still stood, and it seemed best to do likewise.

There was an almost inaudible rustling behind him, and he turned to see a woman entering the room. So tall was she that she had to lower her head for the door that Coyote had passed through unbending, and so thin that she looked like an animated walking-stick. She was dressed all in purple: a narrow purple skirt to her ankles and a purple cape, and her hair hidden by a purple cap fit tightly to her head. The cap's pointed peak did nothing to give her a less forbidding aspect.

"Citizens," she said. "Please sit down."

Coyote gratefully took a chair, and the others did the same, and they sat there gazing politely at one another until Agamen Cady summoned the tray of drinks and did the honors.

The drink was something new to Coyote, and had an effect he noted for future wariness. Never accept two of whatever-this-was.

"An excellent drink, Citizen Cady," he said enthusiastically. "It is called—?"

"That one," answered Cady, "is called 'Golden Flute.' The principal ingredient is fruit juice."

"And the other ingredients?"

Cady chuckled. "A local beverage called lasterfa," he said. "Very potent."

The woman spoke then, rebuking Agamen Cady in a high reedy voice that betrayed how many dozens of cosmetic injections lay behind the elegant unlined face.

"Agamen," she said. "It is typical behavior to open a

meeting by serving one's guests a strong drink, but its typical-
ness in no way diminishes its stupidity. How do you expect
Citizen Jones to follow our discussion?''

Agamen Cady looked fixedly at his silver slippers and
muttered, and the woman reached up to touch the dot on the
ceiling. When it glowed, she said, ''Send us a carafe of
strong coffee at once. *Strong* coffee.''

The wall-niche opened immediately, a carafe of jetty fluid
floated over to them, and she retrieved it neatly from the air
and poured Coyote a sizable cup.

''This sort of bouncing up and down is very bad for the
metabolism,'' she said, handing it to him, ''but your present
state of euphoria would be even worse for the work that needs
to be done. Drink this, please.'' And turning to Cady she
said, ''And you, Agamen Horta, no further displays of silliness.
We have much to talk about.''

Coyote looked at the ceiling, took deep breaths, and waited
until the room became its stark and sterile self once again.

''Better?'' asked the Reverend Rabbi-Pastor.

''Yes,'' said Coyote. ''Unfortunately.''

She scowled at him, narrow high-arched black brows meeting over the pointed nose, and raised one index finger like a
needle higher than her head.

''Alcoholic drinks,'' she said, ''are a frivolous waste of
time. I should be disappointed to learn that a Student would
indulge in such trivia.'' And before he was able to disabuse
her of her illusions by letting her know how deeply attached
he was to just the kinds of trivia she so deplored, not to
mention a number of others he was reasonably sure she would
look upon with equal lack of favor, she brought the meeting
to order, opened it, took the floor, and stated the first item on
her agenda.

''I,'' she said, ''am the Reverend Rabbi-Pastor Sarah Dorcas Elimalek, supreme official of the Church of the Old
Faith. Fortunately these are my official names, something
you will have guessed by their cumbersome absurdity, and
you may address me simply as Reverend, or, for that matter,
as Citizen Cady. In ordinary terms I am Agamen's oldest
sister, Fara Cady. I go through this tedious recitation in order

to provide you information relevant to your studies, Citizen Jones."

"Thank you, Citizen Dady," said Coyote. "Every little bit helps."

"We are informed by Multiversity Two that your doctoral dissertation is to be on the subject of our little domestic religious revolt, Citizen, and we are of course extremely flattered. We must insist, however, that you abide by the terms of the agreement with our government and conceal the name, location, and physical geography of this planet, Not that the word of a Student is ever in question, but I want to be certain that there is no misunderstanding."

"You need not be concerned," said Coyote, his face registering, he hoped, polite and shocked distaste for this superfluous caution. "In my dissertation the planet will be named with a number, located beyond the Extreme Moons, and described as a barren waste. I promise you."

She nodded at him, the sharp face showing pleasure. "Very well, then," she said, "those terms having been made explicit, we are most anxious to be of service to you . . . and, for you to be of service to us."

"*That* in particular," said Agamen Cady, who was busily engaged in pouring a new set of drinks, presumably nonnarcotic this time. "That in particular."

Coyote was not at all sure what would come next, especially since he was facing not an amateur in religion, but an expert. He did his best to look completely confident, and asked, "And in just what way can I be of use to you, Citizens?"

The woman leaned forward and clasped her thin hands in front of her. The intensity of her gaze inspired no euphoria whatsoever.

"We need information," she said, "and we need it badly."

"Surely your computers provide you with ample information?" he said, surprised.

"Not the sort we need."

"You see," put in Agamen Cady, "the computer gives us statistics." He rubbed furiously at his nose with the back of one languid hand. "How many of our people have defected to this cult in a given week, or day, or hour. What the value of their property might be. The amount of the tithe they would have been paying the Old Faith had they not defected. The amount our operating budget is decreased on any given day by the defections. The number of new dancing-circles constructed by the Shavvies in a given unit of time, and the board-feet of lumber consumed thereby. All that sort of thing.''

''But not what we need,'' the Reverend Rabbi-Pastor said. ''What we need to know is *why*. We need to know what it is in this woman Drussa Silver's religious techniques that makes her so effective. We need observations about the state of mind of new converts—are they wavering at first? Are they absolutely certain? Could they, given a concentrated effort, be won back? We need data about the Silver's tricks, this garbage of so-called miracles and wonders. We need *social* data—what does the new culture of this group offer our people that the Old Faith does not?''

''You want to know how to compete with it,'' Coyote said flatly.

''Exactly!''

''We've managed to infiltrate the group, of course,'' put in Agamen. ''That was simple. But the information coming back is of no use to us. We need an expert.''

Fara Cady looked down at a card on the table before her, and then back at Coyote.

''Our information is that your undergraduate work was in Religious Anthropology, your graduate in Religion, and your specialty Religious Cultural Systems. Correct?''

''Correct.''

She gave a long satisfied sigh, made a steeple of her fingertips, leaned back in the chair, and beamed at him. ''You should be able to help us greatly then,'' she said. ''And we are honored that you are willing to do so. Now . . . how can we be of service to *you* in your work?''

''I also need information,'' said Coyote. ''Everything you can give me. Any detail, no matter how trivial it may seem to you, might be important. I need all the computer printouts. I need to see whatever films you may have made. I need access to all research done by your people.''

"Done."

"And an introduction. I need to be able to move freely among these people."

"Done and done!"

The Reverend Rabbi-Pastor leaned toward him once again, and he resisted the impulse to lean away. It was impossible not to feel that she might topple over on you, so tall and thin and imposingly Gothic was she. He could understand how she inspired obedience in the unsophisticated. If he wasn't very careful, she was going to inspire obedience in *him*.

"As a beginning," she asked him, "would you like to watch one of their so-called worship services?"

"Is that possible?"

"Nothing simpler," she said, and touched a stud on the wall behind her. At once there was a soft hiss, and the wall across from him moved smoothly aside to reveal an enormous comset. "Watch the screen at the upper left, Citizen Jones. You, Agamen—move around here between us so that you can see."

There was a flicker, and then the screen cleared.

"The camera," said Fara Cady, "is hidden in the clothing of one of our infiltrators. We don't get perfect reception this way, of course, but it is sufficiently good to give you an idea of what is going on."

"No sound?" Coyote asked.

"Certainly there is sound. Listen, you'll hear the usual nishia-bella grove noises. Birds. Small animals running around in the higher branches. Leaves rustling."

"What the Citizen means, dear sister," put in Agamen, "is that he hears no voices."

The Rabbi-Pastor's eyebrows shot up and her face registered a kind of distaste Coyote hadn't seen in many years. Something, clearly, struck the lady as *nasty*.

"No," she said, looking at the ceiling, "you will hear no voices. These people conduct their entire service in . . . in mindspeech."

"I see."

"Notice the young woman standing at the very center?"

Coyote looked at the fuzzy picture. People, leafy branches.

A nondescript outdoor crowd scene. He waited for her to go
on.

"She is standing at the center of the spiral of inlaid tiles, a
Shavvy symbol that is meant to represent the giant fern. She
is leading the service in mindspeech, and you will hear no
sound until the music begins."

It was a dull spectacle to watch; the leader at the center of
the emerald spiral, and everyone else kneeling on the wooden
platform around her, motionless. It did not exactly grip the
attention.

"Citizen Cady," he asked finally, "is this custom of
conducting the service in mindspeech something the Shavvies
take from the Old Faith; or is it an innovation?"

The old woman shuddered, and he thought for a moment
that she would refuse to answer. Apparently he had struck a
nerve. But she spoke, spitting out her words venomously.

"Citizen Jones," she hissed, "this barbarism they call a
religious service takes *nothing*—nothing at all—from the customs of the Old Faith. There is nothing more repulsive to us
than the idea of worship conducted in mindspeech; it sickens
me even to say those *words!*"

"Oh . . . may I ask why?"

"Why!" Her voice went shrieking upward with outrage.
"You, of all people, ask me that?"

"I beg your pardon, Citizen?"

She thrust both hands forward, fingers splayed, her face
distorted with emotion. "I understand," she said, "from the
information given us about you, that you were once involved
with a mindwife of the planet Abba, Citizen Jones. Therefore
you are unquestionably aware of the sickening intimacy
mindspeech makes possible."

Coyote cleared his throat, but she did not allow him to
speak. Who the hell could have been so stupid as to provide
her with that information?

"On this planet," she continued, "as on *any* civilized
world, the use of mindspeech is confined to two situations
and only those two—genuine emergencies, and the necessary
transfer of information through intersteller distances. Just as
there must in every culture be some individuals who concern

themselves with such matters as the disposal of human wastes and the preparation of the dead for cremation, so there must be individuals who use mindspeech, where society requires it. In any other situation we look upon mindspeech as we would upon public defecation.''

"I see," said Coyote. "I understand."

"*Do* you?"

"I think so," he said.

"I think not!" she snapped back. "If you understood, you would not have been able to spend a year among the Maklunites, who I happen to know are also given to this disgusting abuse of the mind. Like communal smearing of feces, Citizen Jones!"

Coyote shrugged. "Since someone has provided you with my life story," he said, "you undoubtedly know also that I failed in my attempt to become a Maklunite."

"Naturally," said Agamen Cady. "No person of even elementary decency *could* succeed."

On the screen the kneeling people were rising, and to Coyote's great surprise, the music that signaled the end of the kneeling sounded like guitar and flute. He could see the musicians, sitting at the far edge of the wooden floor, and he did not recognize the instruments they were holding; but the sound was enough like guitar and flute to fool you if you weren't looking while you listened. The musicians played and the Shavvies danced, and he would have liked to join them. They seemed to be enjoying themselves immensely.

"Reverend Rabbi-Pastor," he said abruptly, "there's something that I do not understand."

"Yes?"

"If the use of mindspeech is a primary taboo among your people, as it appears to be—"

"Certainly it is!"

"—then how does Drussa Silver get them away from the Old Faith? I should think they would be so repelled by the method of worship that the repulsion alone would keep them from converting to the cult."

"Ah, Citizen," she said, "there is nothing in the universe so appealing as forbidden fruit."

Coyote shook his head.

"Just a minute," he said, "I want to be very precise about this. When you speak of 'forbidden fruit,' you are using a phrase usually applied to the breaking of *sexual* taboos. For example, during the twentieth and twenty-first centuries there was truly nothing so deliciously appealing to the people of Old Earth as breaking the taboo of sexual monogamy. But you compared the use of mindspeech to public defecation, Citizen Cady—and that is a very different sort of taboo."

"I fail to see that this kind of subtle distinction—"

"I will need to know," Coyote cut her off, "into which class this mindspeech taboo falls, because it makes a difference."

There was a long silence, broken only by the soft click as the old woman turned off the comset and covered it once again.

"Sister," said Agamen Cady finally, "please do remember that you are speaking to a scientist here, an expert in cultural systems and their religious manifestations. Surely you cannot expect him to accomplish anything useful if we attempt to keep a part of the data from him?"

She stared at him angrily, but he did not drop his glance; this fluffy individual could be quite firm when he felt it to be necessary, apparently.

"Well, Citizen," said the Reverend Rabbi-Pastor.

"Yes?"

"I suppose I must tell you the truth, much as I dislike it."

"If we are to get anywhere with this project, you must."

"Then," she said. "I will have to admit that for the majority of our people today the taboo falls into the class of sexual prohibitions, in your terms. In our larger cities, Citizen, there are prostitutes—illegal, of course, and stamped out by our law-robots as quickly as they are located—who will provide conversation in mindspeech, for a fee."

"For you it is different, however?" Coyote asked gently.

"For me," she said in a thin voice, "there is no more repulsive action that a human being can take. In an emergency, I would certainly prefer death to using mindspeech to call for help."

She stood up suddenly, gathering her cape tightly about her, and Coyote saw the signs of strain on the falsely youthful face. Even the cosmetic injections were not going to be able to maintain her much longer, he realized. She was nearing the age of death.

"This meeting is adjourned," she said. "Citizen Jones, I must tell you that Drussa Silver is not at this moment in our Sector, but is causing her disgusting havoc in the area of Castle Fra, in Sector One. We will see that you are taken there at once and given suitable accommodations at the Castle, and I will arrange for the necessary introductions to allow you to move about freely among the Shavvies. Perhaps at *last* we will make some progress!"

"I sincerely hope so, Citizen," Coyote murmured.

"And you, Agamen, will go at once to the Third Tower, where there is a stack of business messages waiting for your attention. Come along, Citizen Jones!"

He followed her, hoping. But she remembered to duck her head before going through the door.

Chapter Six

> Friend, your mind has betrayed you.
> On the back of your eyes
> it shines lies and says "It's real! It's real!
> Go out and die for it!"
>
> How can I teach you that moments are counted in
> hundreds of years?
> You have trapped your self in a now
> you cannot see past.
>
> It has no truth value.
> It is not even an f of an x.
> It rots in your head.
>
> A shut-up winged thing, you beat at your bars.
> I spell a word to free you.
>
> —from *Cornfield Crane*, by
> s.e., a twentieth-century poet

First Journal Entry—November 3030.

My name is Star-Fox and I am in fealty to the noble family of Castle Fra. I live at the edge of the Castle wall, in the corner, so that two walls of my house are the Castle wall itself, and I am my mother's one and only child.

We are fortunate, my mother and I. My father was a playmate of the man who is steward to the Castle Economist, and he was given this house to live in out of friendship and old ties. When he died, the Fra let us remain here. For everyone else, there are the government issue bubble-houses— ugly, serviceable things. For us, we have two walls of real stone—these being the Castle wall—and two of synthostone almost six hundred years old. The post of gatekeeper has been held by the computer for nearly that long, but the house still stands and we live inside.

My mother is called Analyn, and she is a sorceress, a witchwoman, a maker of spells. She has been useful to the Old Faith, which needs her skills of illusion and her powerful Singing. She has done the Singing at the first-day-of-the-month service each and every month for the past eighteen years at Castle Fra. I am proud to be her daughter.

First, the Citizen Pastor gives the signal and the bells are rung until they seem to be ringing inside our heads as well as outside. We kneel, facing the south where the dawn comes, and we all pray together that the sun may rise strong in the southern sky and light our day. A silly prayer, my mother says, but it is the tradition and we all feel comfortable in the saying of it.

Second, the Disc is raised, round and golden and full of a flickering light that hurts your eyes, so that you must not look at it directly but must always look just *past* it if you want to see it, and as it rises the music begins at the back of the Chapel, all the electric notes quivering together toward the top of the roof, high and thin and powerful.

Third, the service, which is dull, dull, dull—my instructions in this journal are that I must tell the truth—with the Citizen Pastor telling us what is expected of us yet one more time.

The duty of a Citizen is to support the state with one-twentieth of hisandher goods, and all that heandshe may earn, and all that shall come to himandher out of the grace and the goodness of the Supreme Being blah blah blah . . .

The duty of a Citizen is to accept those laws and those lines which the state shall lay upon himandher in the exercise of its authority through the eight noble families, and to serve in willingness and blah blah blah blah blah . . .

*   *   *

The duty of a Citizen is to rise before the dawn and prepare himselfandherself to greet the Holy Sun that gives us a long and lightful day in which to labor for blah blah blah blah blah . . .

There are twenty-four duties, the Twice Twelve Duties, and we know them all by heart. By the time we are able to sit at the comset in our infant-chairs, still held up by straps instead of our own spines, we are listening each day and three times each day to the recitation of the Twice Twelve Creed. By the time we must begin tuning in each morning to the edcomputers to be taught, we can say it all, although we have no idea what it means, and at the end of each week when we take the comset stylus to take the tests we can write the Creed as rapidly as the computer can check it. (I am asked to comment, as I write, upon our education. I can only say that this seems to be a silly way to teach anybody anything, because after a year or two the Creed is like the wind, like the beating of our hearts, we no longer hear it. Or perhaps that is what the educators intend?)

Fourth, the collection of our tithes for that week, as each one of us goes to the altar to insert our credit-disc in the Tithing Slot.

Fifth, the presentation of the newborn Citizens and the farewell to the newdead.

Sixth, the formal blessing of the day to come, and the listing of our assigned tasks for that day.

And seventh, my mother does the Singing.

My mother. She goes to the front of the Chapel, to the small Chamber of Glass, and stands where the Disc is suspended, its brilliance above her head and the light it casts making a circle inside which she stands. She is dressed all in cloth-of-gold, hundreds of years old and preserved down the line of Singers by their power only. Across her body, from left shoulder to right hip, is slung the holy Sword, cast in platinum, studded with jewels from hilt to tip, the light leaping off its razor edge and playing among the light from the Disc. It is as if my mother is surrounded by lightnings, where she stands.

She closes her eyes and waits for the Sun to flood into her, while all of us, all we ordinary people who cannot Sing, breathe in holy meditation and watch her grow more and more golden.

She crosses her hands on her breasts, she places her feet in the sacred positions, she turns slowly twenty-four times round, once for each one of the Duties, she seems to grow more and more tall with each turn . . . at the last she is a column of flame.

(There are times when I wonder, although such wondering is perhaps wicked, if everyone sees this, or if it is only we young ones. Perhaps the grownups, watching a Singer year in and year out, twelve times each year on the first-day service, half a dozen times more during the Highlidays, become bored with it all? Perhaps they see only a woman, wearing an ancient dress and a sword that is too heavy, going through rituals that have no magic left for them?

This is possible, of course. When I was a very tiny girl, I believed, with my whole heart, in the emerald spirits no longer than my littlest fingernail who are said to live in the spirals of the giant fern. I saw one once, I thought, perched in the turn of a young frond. I am aware now that I saw the insect that feeds on the fronds at that time of the year, but at that moment I *saw* the emerald spirit, as I now see my mother become a column of light and flame.

If it is like that, if I will outgrow what I now see in Chapel when my mother Sings, then I sorrow for that and will fight it when it comes.)

When my mother is there in the Chamber of Glass, there is no sound anywhere, not a whisper of breath, not a murmur. Her beauty hushes even the babies back of the soundbaffle, and then, ah, then she begins to Sing.

I cannot write very clearly about the Singing. How could I describe it? You would have to hear it yourself. My mother Sings the holy sounds of the Three Kinds . . . Submission, Serenity, and Service. There are no words to these Songs, they are not like the songs of popular musicians; but they speak clearly to us, and they braid our spirits neatly for the coming month. While my mother Sings there is no time, there is almost no breathing, and the holy sounds take you out of yourself, bringing a peace, a bliss, a need to begin again in the work that you have been given to do . . . poor words. Only if I could Sing would I be able to make it clear, and then the words wouldn't be needed, for I could simply Sing to you.

I had thought that I might be a Singer. I prayed for it, when I was small, and when I knew it wasn't going to happen, I wanted to die. But something else is intended for me, I believe, and although it is not Singing it is important. It appears . . . I am almost afraid to set it down here, for fear it will tempt some fate to take it away from me . . . it appears that I am going to Multiversity, that I will be a Student. There—I've said it.

All the billions of children, through three galaxies, sitting down every morning to do their lessons with the edcomputer. Out of all those billions, only one thousand can be chosen to study with a *living* Teacher, to be in classrooms with other Students, to go to school, real school. They say now that I will be one of the thousand. They say that a place will be set aside for me so that when I reach the age of sixteen I will leave here and go to become one of the thousand.

We shall see. Perhaps I will not continue to do so well. Perhaps the edcomputer will stop sending through the profiles marked MULTIVERSITY POTENTIAL TOP PRIORITY and send the other kind . . . SATISFACTORY. OR COULD DO BETTER WORK IF MORE EFFORT WAS PUT FORTH. OR A VERY STUBBORN AND DISPLEASING CHILD—PUNISHMENT INDICATED. And if that happens, surely I *will* die, this time, of heartbreak and disgrace. Only two more years, now, until I am sixteen, and they are so sure that now I have been asked to keep the journal required of all MULTIVERSITY POTENTIAL students. How would I feel at sixteen to be refused, to have the journal taken away for study, for analysis of my failure, to try to find out where the potential went? They say that almost never happens, that the edcomputers do not make mistakes, but I am afraid. I am afraid that perhaps my fear *indicates* that this is one of the rare mistakes. It seems to me that I should be more confident, somehow.

Mother will not speak of it at all. She says we must not. We must not count on my going to Multiversity; we must assume I will grow up and marry one of the men chosen for me by the Citizen Pastor as husband-candidates, and live out my life in this Sector, in a bubble-house with two extruded bedchambers and walls of a poisonous mauve.

At the prospect I am sick and weak and I feel my mind dull in its bony coverings and shrink into itself. You see that I cannot afford the luxury of discouragement.

We are to write down everything we can, they say. The word they use is "copiously"; we are to write copiously. The more we write, the better they can prepare for us our program of study, the better utilization can be made of our potential as Students. I understand that and see it as an obligation, as does the Citizen Pastor, obviously, since he has released me from three hours of other duties to do this writing.

But I am growing tired. The writing process does not suit me. Numbers are *my* function, the elegance of them weaving in and out of their patterns, the beautiful names of them . . . dodecahedron, tesseract, tri-tesseract-anapsis, cube and line, sine and root . . . I have a language made only of numbers and their grave and delightful names, and its grammar is formed of its own fitness, without need for all this fat that you have when you deal with words. Words are sloppy, untidy, flopping-about things, and I dislike and distrust them.

But I must set down here what happened yesterday at our house, it is my duty to do so. It was such a strange thing, and well worth noting.

Just before the noon tea, when I was in the kitchen-alcove trying to coax our cranky old Nutrirobot to produce something fit for human beings to eat, there was a feeling that came suddenly and encircled our house. Like a questing . . . like something seeking us out and warning us of its coming.

My mother went quickly to let Drussa Silver in, where she stood waiting at our stone-framed door, and she did not seem in the least afraid. I was afraid, because it is very near to treason to have that woman in a house of the Old Faith, but of course a Singer need not fear anything or anyone. Still, my hands were cold and my breath came fast in my throat; and if my mother had not told me sharply to stay where I was, I would have run out of the house.

She is called Drussa Silver, but she is a woman of gold, not silver. She is tall and slender and has glowing brown silken skin that draws your fingers toward it, you want so badly to touch it. She wore a tunic of pale wheat color with a border of the deep green the Shavvies use so much—the color of the giant ferns they border their dancing-circles with—and her feet were bare, her gold-brown hair in two thick braids like all the Shavvy women. And she was beautiful, of a beauty that made the air about her beautiful and shed light on our housewalls and was like a note of music in the rooms. My mother is beautiful only when she Sings, but this woman was Singing just by her presence, and beautiful in and of herself.

She came in and sat down on the stone ledge beside our front door, and for a few minutes she said nothing, only looked around her, looking at me where I stood frozen in the kitchen alcove, and looking at my mother, who was calmly looking right back.

YOU ARE THE SINGER, she said then, her mindvoice cool and scented of the black loam beneath the nishia-bella trees. My face went hot and I gasped aloud, because only prostitutes behave in that way, but my mother answered as if mindspeech were as common in our house as bread and takkafruit.

I AM ONE SINGER OF MANY, she said, and I blushed for her.

YOU ARE THE ONE WHO IS NEEDED, ANALYN, said Drussa Silver, and my mother's eyes widened, and she said, NEEDED? AND HOW AM I NEEDED?

There was a mindsound of wind and water, an image of iris unfolding purple and crisp and flecked with gold fur at the throat, spiked green leaves studded with dew, and Drussa Silver spoke again.

ANALYN OF FRA, WHEN THE TIME COMES YOU WILL KNOW.

I AM NOT NOBLY BORN, said my mother. I AM A COMMON WOMAN OF THE COMMON PEOPLE. I SERVE THEM AND THE NOBLE FAMILIES IN THE ONLY WAY I KNOW.

Drussa Silver smiled then, and for the first time she spoke aloud.

"Nobility," she said, "is an inner thing. It has nothing to do with bloodlines and marriages."

"What will be asked of me? And by whom?"

I saw now that my mother was beginning to be afraid, and the walls closed in around me. She is my rock, and I had never seen her afraid of anything before—not even when the deadly snakes came after the last seaflood and our floor was alive with them. Drussa Silver raised one hand beside her face, her fingers arranged in the Teacher's gesture, though she is no Teacher. "There is an ancient line," she said softly. *"Of one unto whom much is given, much shall be required.* The equilibrium of the universe does the requiring, Analyn of Fra, that the delicate life-balances may be maintained."

This I understood; it is mathematical. However, I have yet to see it demonstrated in the world around me. Everything is given to the noble families, of whom very little is required.

She spoke to me, then. "You, child," she said, "you will help your mother. There are days coming soon when she will be at the storm's center, and only she will have some power over the forces that shake this world. When that time comes she will need you beside her, and when you go away, she will need your learning and your thoughts. It is a solemn obligation, and it will be heavy upon you."

I could not help what I did, I fell to my knees before her because her eyes compelled me, and I heard the indrawn hiss of my mother's breath. We of the Old Faith kneel only to the Sun, and to no human born—not even to the Reverend Rabbi-Pastor. But I had no more power than a creature struck down, and I was glad to kneel.

"That was a cheap trick," said my mother, lashing out at the holy woman, "and it is a good thing you use it on a child! Only a child would be impressed."

I saw a look cross Drussa Silver's face, a look of sorrow and of one heavily burdened; and then, while I looked out from behind my trembling hands, she turned those eyes on my mother.

It was as well that I was kneeling already, for I would have fallen in any case. The room was whirling around me. My mother grasped the frame of the door and held it, and I saw the cords stand out in her throat, saw her whole body shudder as she fought the swirling of power all about us, and I heard her cry out in despair. And then she knelt, too, compelled as I had been, Analyn the Singer on her knees before this woman who had come to tear away the accustomed fabric of our lives.

It stopped, as a wind ceases sometimes to blow, and it was Drussa Silver who went to her knees, beside my mother. Her voice was like cool water on a burn, and she spoke close to my mother's ear so that I could scarcely hear.

"I must show you something," she said. "I must, because you are going to be sorely needed, and because you are the only one strong enough to bear it. I am going to show you what is *real*, Analyn the Singer, so that you will remember it forever, and so that this dream-structure set up by human beings cannot ever again confuse you."

My mother was trembling. I could not bear to see her so; when Drussa Silver stood up I ran to my mother and put my arms around her to still her shivering.

LOOK THERE, said the holy woman, AND LOOK WELL.

My mother's body went rigid as stone in my arms, and I saw her eyes grow wide and a distance come in them. My heart pounded in me, but hers had stopped at what she saw.

As for me, I saw nothing, because the world tipped once and went black around me. I heard my mother say—or perhaps I heard her Sing—"Forgive me," and then the words of the woman called Silver, in my mind.

IT IS I WHO MUST BE FORGIVEN, FOR THE THINGS THAT I HAVE NO CHOICE BUT TO DO.

And then I knew nothing more. When I came to myself I was on my bed, and my mother bending over me, and Drussa Silver had left our house.

When I tried to speak, Mother hushed me. "Truly," she said, "now is a time when you must keep silence, child."

I do not know what to think of all this. A Singer is not humbled by anything ordinary. And yet Drussa Silver is a known sorceress, a woman who has tempted millions of our people away from the Old Faith with her trickery. All of us know the tricks a person of strong psibility can play on others, and the Silver woman was for all the years of her childhood at the Communipath Creche, a potential candidate for the post of message-channel to Three Galaxies. Who knows what sort of deviltry she may not have learned there? And it is known that she was released from the Creche as unfit for service, surely a sign of great wickedness—though when she was near me I thought only that she was holy.

I am going back to my equations, where things behave as they *ought* to behave, and where one thing follows from another in elegance and rigor. My mother will not speak of the Silver's visit, or of what happened. She said only, "I am bruised of spirit . . ." and has said nothing since. She talks of our house, and of my behavior, and sometimes she speaks of the small garden we keep along our side window. She spends much time walking, high in the nishia-bella trees, even when the upper branches are lost in fog and rain; and she comes home soaked through to the flesh, with a look in her eyes that I have never seen before.

I can only wait and see what will come to pass.

Chapter Seven

You will maintain in your reports at all times the cumbersome style developed by the linguistics computers through analysis of the educational literature of 20th-century Old Earth. This style, which was characterized by an almost total lack of semantic content, lends itself superbly to adaptation for coded messages. (In addition, since it is used nowhere else, it serves to identify agents' messages in cases where they are lost, misplaced, or stolen.)

—*Manual of the Tri-Galactic Intelligence Service, p. 4*

FILE : 1304.a, Segment 2
TOPIC: MISSION FREEWAY, Initial Report
FROM: Citizen Coyote Jones
TO : TRI-GALACTIC INTELLIGENCE SERVICE
GALCENTRAL, STATION FIVE (MARS-CENTRAL)
DATE: Novemberthird 3030

1. I arrived on Freeway one week ago, shortly after dawn, and was landed by Hook, an exotic touch which was somehow not included in my briefing for this mission. As a result, my mood on landing lacked the cheery perfection my friends ordinarily associate with me, and there might well have been an unfortunate intergalactic incident. (This eventuality was aborted by the accidental item that my first on-planet contact was a computer rather than a Citizen.) No doubt steps will be taken in the future to prevent this sort of dangerous failure to supply much-needed information to agents at their premission briefings.

2. I was met by one Agamen Horta Cady, a member of the noble family living in Castle Olyon, Sector Five ("sector" being both a political and a geographical division of this planet), and was taken by him to a meeting with the chief religious official of Freeway. This personage is Agamen's sister Fara, officially known as the Reverend Rabbi-Pastor Sarah Dorcas Elimalek. The woman appears to be of venerable age, despite the effects of cosmetic injections, and is clearly in a position of significant power. The meeting proceeded satisfactorily, and I will provide full details upon my return.

3. The political situation on this planet is one of the Standard Modes—a class-stratified society with a group of "noble families" at the top, a class of civil servants called "fealtors" in the middle, and a mass composed of everybody else at the bottom. The government is pseudo-parliamentarian; there is a Red Council, representing the nobility, a Blue Council, representing the fealtors, and a Green Council representing the average citizen. As would be expected in this primitive Mode, the power is concentrated in the Red Council, although there appears to be no *overt* oppression of the lower classes. The planet is divided into eight Sectors (see #2 above), of roughly equal size, each ruled by one of the noble families. Details are provided at the end of this report.

. Each noble family has a castle in the capital city of its sector, in which the immediate family and innumerable relatives make their residence. Outside the castle proper, but within its walls, are the homes of the fealtors. Outside the castle walls the rest of the population is housed in settlements ranging from small villages to cities of 50,000 or more. Freeway is, as noted in extant documents, a planet of very low population density, a situation not surprising in view of (1) the great difficulty of clearing the nishia-bella groves to provide land for expansion, and (2) the fact that there is essentially only one habitable continent. However, since the beauty of the planet lives up to the extravagant claims made for it in Classified File 10738942, this situation obviously will not outlast the cancellation of its Novice Planet status. The oceans which occupy most of the planet surface will obviously support thousands of floating buckminsters, and I am certain that the immigrants to settle the buckminsters would be in the millions. The current population of Freeway is *not* going to appreciate this growth, and the anticipation of its happening will certainly create great difficulties and delays when termination of Novice status begins. Please see that the relevant fedbureaus are alerted.)

5. A brief architectural remark. The "castles" are a paradigm example of tradition in conflict with progress. On the outside, they are straight out of the ancient Grimm texts, complete with turrets, moats, drawbridges, the lot. There are almost five hundred separate rooms in Castle Olyon, for example, and I am told that it is not the largest of the eight castles. Inside, however, these buildings are like luxury scientific spaceliners, with every need supplied by computers and various servomechanisms. The entire "staff" for such a castle, which must once have involved great numbers of citizens under the supervision of the fealtors, now consists of a single human being known as the Castle Economist. I was not allowed to take photographs, of course, but when I return I will be able to provide data for simulations to be prepared by our art people.

The fealtors live in g-i bubble houses, in the usual depressing colors and styles, as do the masses. The only apparent difference is that every fealtor home is a single-family dwelling while most of the lower rank live in multiple-family communal housing. I have not yet been able to learn whether this is obligatory, a matter of choice, or keyed to the income of the individual.

6. I have now been given housing in one of the guest house attached to Castle Fra, in the sector where Drussa Silver is at this time operating. I have suffered through the usual introductory round of parties and receptions and tours—at none of which, the Light be praised, have I encountered any real expert in Religion—and I now anticipate that I will be able to

begin observing the Shavvies, and Drussa Silver, directly. The noble contingent have made arrangements for me to be accepted, apparently without question, by the people Citizen Silver leads. (I will of course not learn until I actually *try* it whether there is going to be resistance to my "scholarly investigation." At least none was expressed to the nobles, but that probably means just about as much as it would in any society of this primitive type.)

It is important, by the way, that the files in the relevant bureaus be altered to show that the name given this group in my briefing—"Silverites"—is not correct, and is a typical administrative error. The group are properly called *Shavvies,* Panglish-phonemically /shá + viyz/. The term "shavvy" itself is an old slang word meaning "fruitpicker," from the historical period of Old Earth just before all human agricultural workers were replaced by agrirobots. I would suggest that inquiries be made by the Federal Bureau of Linguistics with regard to the possible relationship between the word "shavvy" and the Old Panglish proper name "Chavez," which occurs several times in ancient manuscripts of this group.

7. The Shavvies have been allowed to function undisturbed on Freeway for countless years, exactly as I was advised in my briefing. Their existence as a threat to the established culture, however, which has developed only recently with the emergence of this woman Drussa Silver, is in no way mysterious or obscure, as follows: all members of the establishment religion, a branch of Neo-Judaeo-Christianity called (as usual) the Old Faith, pay a tithe of THIRTY PER CENT of their income to the church. (The "Church" being, of course, the noble families.) The sudden and massive defection of citizens to the Shavvies is not a threat to the religion, it is simply— excuse my departure from the style of the Official Manual For Preparation Of Official Reports—playing hell with the treasury.

8. I have only just begun to accumulate data about the Shavvies, although I have naturally read all the materials provided to me by the Dean at Multiversity Two. One fact

that appears to be sufficiently striking to report at this early date, however, is that one of the defining characteristics of the religion is an *advanced development in telekinesis*. (This is of course an additional similarity between the Shavvies and the Maklunites—see RB Publication 67.3, Chapter 14, for details.) It introduces a complication of some importance, since my task here is—basically—to catch Drussa Silver faking a "miracle" in order to provide some basis for the charge that she is violating Galactic Regulation Seventeen. All of the Shavvies apparently walk on water, disappear and appear by self-teleportation, toss things around by power of the mind alone, and so on. Interestingly enough, they contend that this is perfectly ordinary human behavior, a part of Drussa Silver's teachings on the proper function mode for human beings.

Now, given these conditions, I'm not quite sure what will constitute a "faked miracle." I will assume, for the moment, that what I am looking for is something done by the alleged lady avatar that everyone around me appears to see happening while I see nothing. If this does not seem to TGIS an adequate way to proceed, please advise at once. But it is *crucial* that the techniques this woman uses in her teaching be made available to the staff at the Communipath Creche and perhaps to the mass-edcomputer staffs throughout the Federation. If she is able to increase the telekinetic abilities of these people so drastically, when they are not Factor Q individuals but ordinary people with ordinary psibilities, think what the same techniques might develop in the highly gifted! I suggest that this be given top priority.

9. Further reports will be forthcoming as soon as I have gathered sufficient data.

END OF REPORT

PERTINENT DATA FOR INCORPORATION IN FILES:

CASTLE	SECTOR	FAMILY
Castle Fra	One	Kellyr
Castle Able	Two	Minora

Castle Tenasselle	Three	Bass
Castle Hight	Four	Asodelyr
Castle Olyon	Five	Cady
Castle Bernadette of Pau	Six	Manoux-Gerardain
Castle Helix	Seven	Smythe
Castle Guthrie	Eight	Begaye

NOTE ONE: Why the hell was I not advised that mindspeech is the primary taboo on this planet? You think that's funny? I don't. I didn't think the surprise Hook landing was funny either.

NOTE TWO: No doubt you have by now been advised of my brief detour to the Planet Galoralon. I sincerely hope my performance there was satisfactory to everyone?

II

Darling Ratha,

I'm glad now that I didn't try to bring you along, love. This trip has turned out to be a lot more exciting than I had thought it would be, and some of it wouldn't have been pleasant for you. I'm sorry, though, that you can't see the planet where I am staying, because it's beautiful. Can you imagine trees so big that people ride little animals, like donkeys, along their branches? And not just children like yourself, darlin'—here the grown-ups spend as much time up in the trees as they do on the ground. When I get home I'll tell you all about it.

I've been spending my time with interesting people . . . though I expect you'll be ashamed to hear that I spend most of *my* time on the ground. I'm not comfortable wandering around hundreds of feet up in the air without so much as a string to hold on to. They tell me nobody ever falls, and that's nice. But I keep thinking I might, and that's not.

Anyway, yesterday I was watching a group of these people

working in a Shavvy garden. (They're very polite about letting me follow them around and watch the things they do.) They were using old-fashioned pyro-ceramic hoes, hand tools, things like that. So what do I do? (Care to guess?) Right. My best Ugly-First-Galaxer act. I made a little speech about how much more efficient it would be if they'd use power tools like everybody else on their planet does, or the servomechanisms that are all over the place. And a lot of other things along the same line.

Well, they looked at me, and they looked at each other. As I said, they're very polite, and they set down their hoes and folded their hands, and then the hoes started racing up and down the rows all by themselves. The vegetables came flying out into baskets, the baskets loaded themselves into wheelbarrows, and the wheelbarrows took off for the storage buildings. Me, I'm standing there watching all this, but I still didn't get it—I was thinking about some kind of new fancy gadget—so they made it absolutely clear for me. They picked *me* up, dumped me into a wheelbarrow, raced me up and down a row or two, and then unloaded me back where I'd been standing. All without ever coming near me, or laying a finger on me. All very gently. The point—which I finally got—was that if they were after efficiency, they sure didn't need any machines to help them get it. I felt pretty silly and pretty stupid, but it was interesting.

And I've met a girl named Deliven, only five years older than you, that I'm anxious to talk to you about. She's something like a child, and something like a princess, and some like something I can't figure out at all. Maybe you'll be able to help me.

I'm bringing you a present, just because I love you, and I'm bringing Tzana Kai a present for putting up with you while I am away. If I'm in a good mood, I may even bring a present or two for your gaza hounds. You tell Tzana Kai hello for me, and do the best you can to be a satisfactory person, even without me around to be your model. (*Don't* tell Tzana Kai I said *that!*)

Bless you, love . . .
Coyote

Chapter Eight

Once upon a time there was a woman who believed that the Sun rose when her husband got up in the morning, and that it set when he came home for his evening meal. The husband was careful to time his activities to fit her belief, although he often found it very inconvenient.

At last, as one might have expected, a day came when the husband was unavoidably delayed and did not come home until almost five o'clock in the morning. To his astonishment, he found that all the flowers in his front garden were shriveled and dead. He went around to the back of the house and found that his vegetables were in the same condition.

"Wife! Wife!" he shouted, wringing his hands in his distress. "Some terrible plague has struck our gardens during the night!" The woman looked at him in amazement, shaking her head. "Why, husband," she asked mildly, "what did you expect, with the Sun blazing down on them all night long?"

—Shavvy teaching fable

It had been a very pleasant week indeed. Coyote had enjoyed himself thoroughly. The Shavvy woman assigned to him as guide had taken him everywhere, and shown him everything, and they had gotten along like old friends. She had taken him to see a Shavvy altar-maker at work and had sat with him explaining each step of the process, from the rough hewing of

95

the block of nishia-bella wood, and the hollowing out of a part of the top to hold earth for the planting of the giant fern, to the carving of the Shavvy emblem in high relief on the altar's front face. She had explained the emblem to him—it was the Tree and the Web, along which one Searched and did one's Choosing—and once it was pointed out to him, he saw that it was everywhere—even scratched on the Castle walls.

She had taken him to a Shavvy breakfast in the forest and encouraged him to join in the grave and elegant circle-dances that followed. When he had tripped over his own big feet she had laughed, but she had held his hand tightly and stayed with him when he began again.

She had told him Shavvy stories, pleasant fables about the adventures of pious fools all come to grief in the end, or puzzle stories where one meaning was hidden inside another and that one in yet another until his head ached. She had sung him Shavvy songs; long, intricate ballads that told stories or hid the instructions for the Shavvy telekinetic techniques, and simple hymns of utter ecstasy.

She had taken him down to the ocean's edge to sit on the sand and watch while Drussa Silver, surrounded by dozens of her flock in holiday tunics, had danced those same circle-dances far out on the surface of the waves, as unconcerned by the fathoms of water beneath their feet as he was by the tons of earth on which he stood. He had sat fascinated, watching them, too awed even for envy, thinking how like magnificent great birds of plumage they looked, dipping and bending among the waves in their tunics of emerald green and deepest azure blue. When the sun struck them, gold shattered against them again and again, like a gong of light, and broke into a million coin-flecks on the water.

He had even tried, when his guide teased him, to go out onto the water himself, and had gotten thoroughly soaked in the course of his foolishness, so that both he and the woman had finally rolled helpless with laughter through the surf like children and ended up on the beach covered with salt and sand and ropes of seaweed. They had been miserable when it all dried out, his hair and beard had been like a helmet of itching brass, and he had never had so welcome a bath as the one that followed that expedition. But it had been worth it.

Everything about their time together had been a delight, up to this moment. He had learned enormous amounts about the Shavvies, solemnly taking miles and miles of scholarly notes, he had had tremendous fun, and he had not had one moment's unease. Up to *this* moment. Now he stood and stared at her, and he had no idea what he was going to do next.

It wasn't that he was unaccustomed to having women ask him to take them to bed. He was fully accustomed to that. He was accustomed to giving a straightforward yes or a straightforward no, and when it was yes he was accustomed to seeing to it that they didn't regret having asked him. What he was *not* accustomed to was hemming and hawing and shuffling his feet like a ten-year-old caught wetting his bed, which was what he was doing now.

"Citizen," the woman said to him, her face betraying her own bewilderment at his behavior, "whatever is the matter? You need only say no, and we'll spend this evening in another way. It's not important, my friend—don't distress yourself so!"

Coyote swallowed hard and tried to think of some graceful way to do this. Worst of all was the idea that she might be feeling that he just pure and simply didn't want her, and that wasn't true. She was a lovely lady, and he was honored by her invitation. But there was a certain problem of self-image here that wasn't easy for him to handle.

"Citizen?" she asked wonderingly. "Have I offended you? Perhaps your customs in these matters are different. . . ."

And that did it. Bedamned with his self-image; he couldn't have her thinking she was in some way at fault.

"Look here," he said slowly, "I'm honored. I'm delighted. You must realize that loving you would be such a pleasure for me. . . . The problem is not in what I want to do, but in what I am *able* to do."

He saw her eyebrows go up, and went on hastily.

"No, no," he assured her, "it's not like it sounds. The difficulty is . . . blast it all, Norda, I'm too old and too set in my ways to take up loving ladies in a synthowood box seven

by five by three-and-a-half feet! Not only am I not sure I'm
capable of the gymnastics involved, I'm not sure that claustro-
phobia wouldn't put an end to the whole thing before it even
got started. There've been a few episodes in sleeping bags in
my time, and one interesting sequence in a rocket ejectopod,
but in all those cases I was out under the open sky, you see.
Confined, yes, but confined in the open. This other business
is something—"

She was laughing, and he didn't blame her. He sounded
like a comset massplay, with some fool dithering about not
being in the mood unless the bedsheets were pink.

"I know," he said miserably. "I do know how ridiculous
it sounds, but do you really want to chance it? Assuming I
have the guts even to try after all this preliminary speech-
making?"

She stepped right up to him, took his hands, and drew him
close, her eyes dancing.

"Coyote Jones," she said, "you are worrying about a
non-problem."

"I assure you—"

"Stop!"

He stopped.

"Do you think," she asked, still laughing, "that we Shavvies
sleep in those grotesque banks of furniture drawers? We don't
use the sleeping-slots, Citizen, we sleep on mats on our
floors, if the weather is bad, and out of doors all the rest of
the time."

"But wait . . . ." Coyote pulled away from her and held her
off gently so that he could think. "What about the ferns?" he
demanded. "What about the infamous narcotic fumes they
give off at night, driving the sleeper mad? I don't think I'd be
much use in an oxygen mask, either, friend, if you want to
know the truth."

"That's all nonsense," she said. "A tale they tell for
children and the ignorant. There's no danger from the ferns—
they give off nothing but their own pure essence and perfume.
The only drugged air on this planet is that piped into the
sleeping-slots."

"You're joking!"

"Not at all." She chuckled and moved back into the circle of his arms, burying her face against her chest. "The air in the sleeping-slots is provided by the central computers as a public utility, and is an integral part of the government's birth-control program. It contains an anaphrodisiac, to keep the population down."

He couldn't believe it. He looked down at the top of her head, took a handful of thick dark braids, and tugged gently. "You are joking," he said again.

"I'm not," she said firmly. "Lie with me, Citizen, and we lie under the stars, out in the forests. Now answer me yes or no, please."

He thought of the miserable nights he'd already spent, shut up like a sardine in a synthowood can. He thought of what he might have missed had she not been a woman of such good sense and patience. And he gave her a fervent yes and followed her off into the sunset, full of a high good humor and ready for *whatever* might need doing.

Chapter Nine

There once was an agent from Saturn
Whose powerful brains made his hat burn;
While the fire-robots sprayed,
His Bureau Chief prayed,
"May his scalp ways more fireproof
than *that* learn!"

> —Anonymous (naturally), circa
> 2929; often shouted in unison
> at the end of TGIS staff parties

He *should* have known. He realized that, afterward, when it was too late. If he'd done his homework properly, read every word of the Shavvy holy books as he ought to have done, he'd have had plenty of warning. As it was, he'd only skimmed a lot of it—especially that portion called the *Book of Prophecies*—because there were few things that bored him much more than religious language. Laziness—that's all it had been—and he had nobody but himself to blame.

Well, perhaps not entirely himself. There was, after all, the fact that this whole assignment was entirely outside his sphere of either training or experience. He was no scholar, although he could manage the jargon of official reports, after a fashion, and he was no diplomat. His ordinary way of doing a mission— and he was damn good at it—was to throw his mind around and subdue unruly nuisances. All this study and subtlety . . . it was like asking him to join a ballet troupe and convince them that he was a ballerina.

What had done him in had been the announcement at the beginning of the Shavvy worship service. He'd been there in the flesh, observing, kneeling at the back of the group in the hope of being a little less conspicuous back there. He could have put on a Shavvy tunic and that would have disguised him somewhat; but it would have been highly suspicious, since the idea of anyone not wanting to be recognized as a Student was totally ridiculous. When only one thousand people out of trillions are allowed to play a particular role, and when new places open in that thousand only when one of the previous thousand completes the course and leaves, you are either proud to be one of the group or you are out of your mind.

And even if he'd been in Shavvy garb it probably wouldn't have helped that much. It was summer, and nobody was wearing the hooded robes, so his hair and beard would have been right out there in front, advertising his presence. Step right this way, folks, and see the Prophecies fulfilled!

He had still not had an opportunity to observe Drussa Silver at close range, although he'd arrived at a dozen places just in time to see her leave. Hoping that she might turn up at the worship-service, and feeling that since she wasn't scheduled to be there she *might* be, he'd gone to the largest service he'd been able to find within walking distance of Castle Fra.

The leader of the service, a man about his own age, had stepped to the middle of the spiral and raised his hands for attention. "Today," he said aloud, "our service will be a little different than usual. We have with us a guest who is mind-deaf; he could not follow our worship in mindspeech. As a courtesy to him, then, we will worship aloud this day."

Not one head turned to look at him. Not one eye turned to stare at the freak in their midst, although they had to have known that he was the guest, the way he stood out in his tattoos. They had gone right on looking at the leader of the service.

They'd started with a passage he recognized. It was the Shavvy Creed, chanted in unison, and like all such sequences of language, so far as he was concerned it was essentially without meaning, full of ponderous gobbledygook. A kind of heavy-breathing pompous paradoxical wordstuff that put you to sleep with its opacity. The sun spattered down through the nishia-bella above their heads, and the giant ferns swayed in the wind, and he was lulled and vulnerable.

"I am a Child of Light," it began.

"Therefore,
I have the power to Search.
Trees of probability make up my life;
I have the power of Search along their branches.

I am a Child of Light.
Therefore,
I have the power to Choose.

Webs of chance make up my life;
I have the power to Choose among their pathways.
Every Choice begets another Choice.

I am a Child of Light.
Therefore,
it is my role to move with power along the time-trees,
along the golden space-webs that span time.

To a Child of Light, nothing can simply 'happen.'
Not to one whose eyes Search, and whose mind Chooses,
for truly such a one creates the passing days
and is ruled by neither space nor time nor any living creature,
nor by any phantom of the spirit,
nor by emptiness."

They'd just begun the final line, "Come then, and make your place here, at my side," and he was very nearly asleep, what with the heavy scent of the ferns, and the hypnotic golden patterns of the leaf-broken sunlight, and the birdcalls, and the droning recitation of the sacred gibberish, when he realized that a group of young boys had moved in to block him off from the rest of the group. After that, things happened so rapidly that he had no clear memory of their sequence. There had been a sensation of rapid flight, a view of trees around him, and then he had begun to spin, faster and faster and faster yet, until the world had blurred, and gone black. . . .

He certainly should have known. The relevant verse was right there in the book, for anyone to read. Chapter 7, Verse 13. "And a cripple will come from another world," it read, "and his beard shall be the color of fire. He will wear the garments of one who desires to learn, but his mind will be like a stone, and his coming shall be a sign and a potent of great sorrow unto the Children of Light." And there he stood, in his Student disguise, red beard flaming away, while his mind-deafness was announced to the group assembled. It would have been quicker and less complicated to have just jumped off the edge of Harvard and terminated his assignment right there.

For a long time—eons of time—he was incredibly busy, while Creation rippled around him and he lay fascinated with its least detail.

He was wrapped in a rainbow, and there were choirs singing to him; except that they sang not notes of sound, but chords of color, and the colors were not ones he had seen before in this universe. From time to time bevies of silver birds circled round him, their wings the windblown prairies for enormous herds of tiny jeweled horses no bigger than his thumb, pounding up over the mountains of birdbacks and down the other side, with their spangled bridles trailing through the silver feathers . . . from time to time, as the birds flew close, they would make charming leaps from the birds into his beard and gallop down onto his chest, where they tickled delightfully. He could not move—he had misplaced his body somewhere and was continually in the process of melting and flowing, but that didn't bother him. Nothing bothered him— not the pyramids of golden roses that formed with a single magnificent burst, not the glorious and beautiful women who melted and flowed right along with him and told him curious ancient tales that he was convinced contained the secrets of the universe. Not the cliff that he became and over which a river flowed, crashing into the depths below and breaking up into something not-quite-spray and not-quite-flower and not-quite-notes, only to race up the cliff and flow over it again. Not the voice that spoke to him from out of a whirlwind of scarlet cinnamon-smell in the key of E minor, and whose words were as soft upon his not-flesh as milkweed down.

None of it bothered him. He had a wonderful time and enjoyed himself hugely. He could have spent the rest of his life (or whatever it was) doing just what he was doing (or whatever it was) without the slightest regrets. Even being sucked backward at the speed of stars out into blinding golden light and tossed again and again into infinite space didn't bother him. He laughed, and bounced from star to star, and waited to be tossed just one more time.

It was not until it was all over that he began to feel uncomfortable, and even then he was not all *that* uncomfortable. He woke up in a drawer just big enough for one-and-a-half people, between two clean sheets, with his loin-cloth and all his tattoos and his shoes neatly hung in a small net bag on a hook beside his feet. Before he discovered that the drawer had a top and that it was only a couple of feet over his head, he tried to sit up, and the resulting thump brought a sudden scurry of feet, followed almost immediately by the drawer sliding out into an enormous room and its side dropping to admit the young woman who had undoubtedly saved him from an intergalactic incident to end all intergalactic incidents.

She slid in beside him and touched him in half a dozen places with a small crystal rod, each touch causing a tone to sound and provoking a satisfied nod from her.

"Good," she said crisply, giving him a look of qualified approval, "you are sufficiently recovered to get up and discuss this disgraceful situation."

She blurred for a moment and then slid into focus, and he recognized her at once.

"You," he marveled, "are—"

"Deliven Kellyr," she said, chopping him off in midphrase. "Yes, indeed. You met me at the Castle Reception just after your arrival in the Sector, and I found your conversation of some interest, since I had not met an offworlder before, much less a Student. That, however, does not explain or excuse your behavior since we met, Citizen."

His behavior. He thought about it. That might involve a number of things. Rape. Murder. Robbery. He might have gone to the center of City Fra and driven the populace mad collectively. Or he might have been more selective and driven only the various government officials mad by convincing them that they were lemmings and must flee into the sea. . . . Under the circumstances, he felt that silence was the only possible course, and he contented himself with clearing his throat and looking as innocent—and as weak—as possible.

Deliven Kellyr slipped out of the drawer as neatly as she had slipped in, and leaned over to deliver her parting message. "Your clothing is there at your feet," she said, "and I would appreciate it if you would put it on. You are quite clean, I assure you, as I have been taking excellent care of you during your . . . episode . . . but if you feel the need of any kind of refurbishment, it is available. You are in a guest-chamber— rarely used, thank the Rings—in Castle Fra, and there is a tiringroom just to your right as you reach the chamber door. I will wait for you in the antechamber. Please be prompt."

And she was gone.

When he joined her, the ground still seemingly rippling under his feet, she was seated at a desk in the antechamber with her hands folded neatly in her lap and an expression of restrained irritation on her face. He slipped into the chair facing her, noted that she had provided coffee, and waited for whatever was going to happen next.

"Well, Citizen," she said at once, "I assume that you would like to know what you have been doing for the past day or two."

He looked humble. He positively radiated humility. A day or two? Great spacehulls . . . great galloping thunder-turtles—a day or two!

"Yes, please," he said.

She whipped a microfiche from the pocket of her skirt and looked at it, whipped it right back, and told him all about it. "You were found," she said, "in *my* personal sleeping-slot, when I returned from evening worship night before last. You were wearing all your clothing, your arms were covered with the glowstamps from the most disgusting of our nightspots and bars, you reeked of liquor—very *cheap* liquor—and you were so far gone that I strongly doubt this universe even grossly represented your location.''

"I—"

"Silence!" she snapped. "I am not through, and you are scarcely in a position to quibble."

"Yes, Young Citizen," he said meekly.

"Have you any idea how you got to my rooms?" she asked.

"None whatsoever."

The corners of her lips twitched, and she stared down at the desk, but her voice was icy.

"Don't you think that's a very unlikely story, Citizen Jones?"

"My last memory," he said carefully, "is of being present at a Shavvy worship service. That may be difficult to believe, but it is the truth."

She looked at him then, her eyes dancing. She was going to be a beautiful woman when she grew up . . . when her body grew up to match her mind, that is. There was nothing childlike about the mind that was in that small golden head.

"I do believe you, Citizen," she said. "I really do. And you will be pleased to hear that you were brought here by a group of five boys, the oldest of whom was fifteen years of age. They got past the computer by the simple expedient of pouring chocolate syrup into the vent guarding this area of the Castle . . . not the kind of thing one expects to have to guard against, and therefore very clever of them. Chocolate syrup!"

She chuckled then, and it was clear to Coyote that she was not really frightened by this gap in the Castle's security system.

"What, exactly, were they up to?" he hazarded.

"The idea was to cause an intergalactic scandal," she said demurely. "You were to be an offworlder who got himself stinking drunk and decided to make free with the body of the daughter of Castle Fra, by hiding yourself in my sleeping-slot and *pouncing* on me when I came to bed."

"I don't pounce," said Coyote crossly.

"They were little boys, Citizen," she rebuked him. "What image do you expect little boys to have of sexual congress?"

Sexual congress? Coyote cleared his throat again and looked at the ceiling.

"Citizen?"

"Yes, Citizen Kellyr?"

"Would you look at me, please? That's better. . . . I dislike having to speak to your beard and that gaudy tropical chest."

"Sorry."

"Well, then. I understand what happened once they had you, Citizen Jones. Their idea was not to do you any physical harm, of course, but simply to embarrass you, tie you up in the intricacies of an interworld diplomatic scandal, make sure that you would be unable to move about freely for quite some time, and generally create a nuisance. The reason the plan failed is quite simple: first of all, they gave you far too much of the narcotic, so that instead of just keeping you euphoric and quiescent until I discovered you, it sent you flying off into the never-nevers. Second, they overdid it, poor babies—*nobody* could put away as much liquor as you were drenched in, or go as many places as you appeared to have gone, and still have the ability to negotiate the Castle ramps and stairs to the sleepingchambers. And finally, they underestimated *me* severely."

"That," said Coyote, "I can believe."

"I was supposed to shriek, scream for my father, and faint dead away, I believe," she said dryly. "A kind of behavior that occurs only in B-grade threedies on vice planets, or in the dreams of teen-age boys."

It would not have been tactful to point out that she was, to his knowledge, only twelve herself. Instead, he asked her what she *had* done, and she ticked it off for him on her fingers.

"One: I made sure the coast was clear to move you. Two: I got three carrying servomechanisms and moved you into the least-used guestchamber. Three: I cleaned you up and made you as respectable as was possible under the circumstances. Four: I obtained a medikit from our storerooms and made certain that you were in no physical danger. Five: I reported to my mother, who took immediate steps to get to the bottom of the incident. Discreetly, of course. Six: I waited for you to come to yourself again. And here we are.''

Coyote sighed. It was not exactly something he could be proud of, being captured and bamboozled by a pack of teen-age religious fanatics.

"Mmmmm," he said.

"Mmmmm? You have nothing else to say? We are holding the—uh, desperate characters—who kidnapped you and brought you here. Would you like to confront them, Citizen?"

"Would I like to what?"

"Citizen Jones!" She was clearly exasperated with him now. "I should like to get this matter attended to, if possible. If you are going to insist on preferring charges, which it is within your right to do, I should like to get on with it."

"Is that what your mother thinks I ought to do?"

"My mother has nothing to do with this, Citizen," she told him, in the voice one uses to address a small child who is being difficult in public. "She is a very busy woman, and she does not concern herself with nonsense of this kind."

Coyote took a deep breath and tried to concentrate.

"Dear Young Citizen," he said solemnly, "if there is one thing I want in all this universe, it is to *not* press charges. The Light preserve me from having to press charges."

"You're certain?"

"Oh, am I certain. Can't you see the headlines now? I can. 'Petulant Religious Expert Trussed and Trounced by Child Fanatics on Interplanetary Junket. Scholars Shocked.' Oh, dear me, child, let's not do that."

"You would not be comfortable with that."

"No. I would not. I would be so humiliated, and so degraded, and so much the laughingstock of Three Galaxies—"

"Citizen Jones," she broke in, "There is something that I *don't* understand."

"And that is?"

"How they got you unconscious in the first place, so that they were able to inject the drugs, plaster you with the nightclub stickers, and bring you here. There is an absolute Shavvy prohibition against violence—how did they manage?"

He told her, and she burst into pealing laughter while he sat and turned redder and redder.

"They spun you, Citizen?" she crowed, choking with laughter. "They spun you! Oh, clever little boys, if only they'd had brains to back up their Shavvy tricks!"

"I'm glad they didn't," said Coyote gravely.

"They would have succeeded, you know," she said, looking suddenly serious, "if only they'd put you into the bed of one of the cousins, or some silly fourteen-year-old serving-woman."

"Probably."

"And you do not want to charge these boys?"

"No," he said. "Not for anything in the world would I have it known that a bunch of kids got the better of me like this. Please."

"What about the consequences of letting their despicable conduct go unpunished?"

"Let it," said Coyote. "Let us only hope they will not brag about it."

"Oh, we will see to that," she assured him. "Set your mind at rest on that score. And I am pleased at your decision."

"Pleased?"

"Yes indeed. There is more than one possible scandal here, you know, Citizen. Can you imagine another headline? How about one on the subject of this Sector's allowing a poor innocent Student to be dragged through the vice pots, disgraced, made a spectacle of, and generally degraded? What about our failure to provide an offworlder—and a scholar at that, and therefore not likely to be accustomed to practical precautions—with the kind of minimal protection we provide our native Citizens? We would not enjoy that publicity any more than you would, Citizen."

He began to see, and he began to feel that he was going to survive this after all, bless her clever kissingerian little heart.

"We are in agreement, then?" he asked.

"In total agreement."

"I am grateful to you for saving my skin, and my image."

"You are quite welcome, Citizen. We are grateful to you for not bringing suit against us."

"Suit against you . . ."

She looked at him with the kind of grave and measuring

attention he associated with medrobots considering the sick. He could hear the wheels whirring in her brain, and then she spoke and made it all quite clear.

"Citizen Jones," she said gently, "you are most incredibly naïve. It is only because I am convinced that you are also incredibly sincere that I am willing to explain to you that you assuredly have an excellent case against our government, if you cared to pursue it. It is our responsibility to *protect* offworlders, who cannot be expected to be aware of the perils of our culture. I was prepared, and am still prepared, to offer you a handsome settlement in exchange for your signature on an agreement not to sue. My mother has authorized a very respectable sum for implementing that agreement."

It was sad. Coyote thought about his own daughter, and tried to visualize her with all these burdens on her shoulders, and he thought it was a damned shame. A child should be thinking of what game to play next, and what delightful investigation of its environment to make next. *Not* intergalactic diplomacy. He was disgusted with a social system that exploited a child in this way and turned her into a precocious bureaucrat and wielder of power.

"You are a very comely man, Citizen Student," she said suddenly, distracting him. "If you are as clever as you are comely, the women who lie with you must consider themselves truly fortunate."

Coyote was startled, mostly to learn that she could still consider the possibility that he was clever. He reviewed his premission briefing on Freeway sexual customs in his head. . . . PLANET FREEWAY: Human Sexual Pattern 11-c, Variation 5, as he recalled. Which meant neither male nor female dominance, sexual relations permitted from puberty and beyond, incest forbidden, homosexuality rare but considered normal . . . followed by a list of what the planetary guardians of morals considered to be perversions. Mostly matters of physical position, if his memory served him right, and naturally lacking the one crucial item: that mindspeech was considered the perversion of perversions.

She was quick. "There is no need for alarm, Citizen," she

said, standing up to look at him sternly. "I would not burden a stranger with a formal invitation from a daughter of Castle Fra; the diplomatic ramifications would be too complicated. I simply believe in giving credit where credit appears to be due."

"I appreciate the compliment," he said. "However undeserved."

"Now," she said, "are you ready to go back to your investigation of Shavvy culture, Citizen?"

Coyote considered it. He held out one hand and watched it shake, put his foot down solidly on the floor and felt it move, and shook his head.

"Not yet," he said. "I need another day to recuperate from that hell's brew they filled me with. Have you a suggestion?"

She frowned slightly.

"Food, first."

"By all means."

"And then . . . is there perhaps something I could do for you? Other than rescuing you from the violence of children, I mean? Have you seen our city? Have you toured the Castle?"

He had it. "There is something you could do."

"Name it."

"You could take me shopping."

"Shopping!"

"Exactly. I want to buy gifts to take home with me, and I don't know your city at all. Since we've struck up an acquaintance . . . after a fashion . . . would you take me around and help me choose something? Do you have time? For that matter, would it be allowed?"

"Allowed?"

She gave him one measuring glance and then shook her head as if his condition were too pitiful to comment on. "Why," she asked, "should I not be allowed to do anything that I considered suitable?"

"There are planets," Coyote told her, "where a girl of twelve would have to ask permission to take an offworld man on a shopping expedition."

Deliven laughed softly, saying, "There are planets where the living process the bodies of their dead for protein. There are planets where infants are raised in complete isolation for the first nine years of their lives. There are planets where all manner of abominations take place. This is not such a planet.''

"Don't you have any rules at all to mind, Young Citizen?'' Coyote asked, thinking of Ratha at twelve and not sure he could face the prospect.

"Three,'' she said promptly. "Don't get up until the Wakers sound, don't neglect my studies, and never fail to be courteous to those around me.'' Then she frowned, and added, "You should remember, Citizen Jones, that we of the Old Faith know quite well what we can and cannot do, from birth. We are not burdened with a lot of troublesome choices, as are the heathens of other planets.''

"Or the Shavvies?''

She shuddered delicately. "It is not in good taste even to discuss those people,'' she said firmly. "And we must be getting started, or there won't be time to do very much.''

About her wrist there was a heavy silver communications bracelet, its various stations marked with small patterned dots of turquoise. She touched the single dot nearest her thumb, and Tayn Kellyr's voice answered, tinny and far away.

"The Student is up and about, Mother,'' said Deliven, "and you will be pleased to hear that he is as unwilling to pursue this matter as we are.''

"Excellent,'' said the tinny voice.

"I am about to take him through the Street of Craftsmen, to choose gifts for taking home to his household. I expect to return in three hours, at the most, and the computers should be advised to expect Citizen Jones as a guest at table this evening.''

"Very good, Deliven,'' said her mother, "I'll see to it.''

Deliven stood up then, and nodded to him, her business with her own household completed.

"Come along, then, Citizen Jones,'' she said, and he followed her meekly out into the corridors, humming an ancient ballad about looking over a four-leaf clover, softly, under his breath.

Chapter Ten

The state of surpassment, in which the spirit moves beyond its ancient boundaries and can no longer be affected by fear or pain or any other illusory perception, comes only with great difficulty to the male human. It is his sorry burden that he can reach this condition only by extended states of deprivation, terror, agony, and the like, inflicted upon him either by himself or by others. It is no wonder, therefore, that primitive man in his consuming jealousy of the ease with which the female could achieve what he did only so rarely and so painfully, did everything he could to conceal her natural abilities away for all time. That he succeeded for so many thousands of years is a tribute to his total dedication to the cause of maintaining this patriarchal myth.

—from *Woman Transcendent*, by Ann Geheygan, p. 44

The woman led him to a clearing in the forest outside City Fra, to a place so silent that his ears hummed with the absence of sound. The nishia-bella trees rose all around him, more like tolerant giant creatures than plants. They had the nobility to keep still and allow the human beings to go about in peace, but Coyote felt their confined power and was nervously aware, here, of their breathing. He had grown accustomed to seeing the people casually riding their animals through the branches as if they were on solid ground, and he had seen groups of fifty or more holding gatherings on the flat places where several massive limbs came together; but when he stepped up into one of them, he always felt as if he should have asked permission first.

A platform had been built in the clearing some three feet off the ground, to clear the stream that flowed beneath it. It had squared-off posts at the corners and down its sides and a slanted roof to let the rain flow down. Shades of some strawlike material were rolled up tight to the roof except on the side from which the wind came most strongly, and there the pale yellow shades fell to the floor.

"She is there," the woman told him, pointing. "She is sleeping."

"At this hour?"

Coyote was amazed. It was an hour past dawn, at least; already the light was beginning to stream down through the cracks in the canopy of leaves and limbs high above their heads. Nobody slept past dawn on this planet, not even the sick. Everyone got up at the Wakers' call and prepared for morning service.

"We are not of the Old Faith," she reminded him. "The Wakers are a convenience for us at times, a nuisance at others, but never a necessity. And Drussa Silver has been struggling all through this night with a group of new converts who torment themselves over shadows; it is difficult sometimes to bring such people into peace with themselves."

"Then perhaps I should not disturb her," said Coyote hesitantly. "What do you think?"

"You must choose for yourself," she said.

"Help me a little, Citizen. I am not one of your people, after all—how can I know your customs?"

She reached over and took his hand in hers and smiled at him. "Come," she said, "we'll go to her, and you will wait beside her till she wakes. I must get back to the City, myself."

She led him up onto the platform, where he saw a dozen people rolled in the light square cloths that Shavvies carried with them wherever they went. They had the property, he was told, of keeping you warm when it was cold and cool when it was hot—not that it ever could be accurately described as hot anywhere but on the small central plains where the nishia-bella did not grow. Everywhere else it was always cool, even at midday.

"There," said the woman, indicating one of the sleeping figures with her free hand. "Sit there beside her; she will wake soon. She never sleeps for long, Citizen."

She was gone before he could thank her, swiftly and so silently that he knew she had not set her feet to the floor or to the ground. Disconcerting, these Shavvy habits—but no doubt very convenient and a big help to the transit bureaus.

He sat waiting for his eyes to adjust to the dimness under the roof, and then at last he had a chance to look at Drussa Silver. He had grown curious, waiting.

He saw that she was beautiful, and he was glad of that. It was old-fashioned of him, but he would have been disappointed if she had been plain. She had gold-brown hair, parted smoothly in the middle and braided in the two long Shavvy plaits, bound with fiber. Her face was oval, her brows perfect, her cheekbones high, her mouth strong and ample and with a delicate curve, and her skin was a pale and rose-flushed brown. One brown arm and shoulder, free of the useful cloth, showed him the fineness of her body, the elegant strength of her hands. He sighed with satisfaction, because all is as it should be when a mythical woman turns out to be of a mythical beauty.

He watched the slow rise and fall of her breasts in the deep breathing of tranquil sleep, and the play of light across her skin when the wind blew the leaves into new patterns. He could have watched her forever in this peaceful place; he was hypnotized by the soft purl of the water flowing beneath him and the dappling of the light. When she spoke, he did not even start, so peaceful had he become.

"Child of Light," she said to him, opening her eyes and reaching for his hands, "you are welcome here, in spite of what you come to do."

He felt the chill of warning and knew he would need to be careful.

"I have come only to learn," he began. "I have—"

"You have come to prove me a fraud and a fake, a corrupter of the innocent, and to take me back to Mars-

Central to be tried in your courts for my life, Citizen Jones. If *you* lie to *me*, however, your own usefulness will be undermined—does the smuggler judge the pirate?''

He was silent, feeling the strong pressure of her hands, trying to think quickly. He had been aware that his cover was weak. But this was total exposure, and it required an adjustment in his plans. But what sort of adjustment? Could she be only trying to trick him into an admission, based on no more than a shrewd and lucky guess?

She let his hands go and sat up, letting the cloth fall away, and in that gesture Coyote lost all the advantage that might have remained to him. He was accustomed to the naked bodies of both men and women. It had been seven hundred years and more since nakedness had been of any importance except on a few isolated planets of the Third Galaxy. But he had never ceased to know joy in seeing a lovely woman naked before him, and this was no ordinary body. Even among the synthetic prostitutes of the vice planets, whose flesh was surgically and chemically made perfect at enormous expense, he had never seen such flawlessness.

"All this perfection is a great nuisance," she said, touching her breasts, "and if it should fade, it would be a lessening of my burdens."

"There is no need for it to fade," said Coyote. "It would be a terrible waste."

"Nonsense," she said, pulling her tunic over her head and letting down her braids to be redone for the day. "If you are talking of cosmetic injections, my friend, I assure you they are not for me. This body is only an encumbrance to me."

"I don't understand," he said, although he understood perfectly well.

"Because," she said, "men desire it. It is natural that they should, I can see for myself that I am very beautiful. But desire is a barrier between me and the spirit of the men I seek to help, even when I am cloaked and hooded. I was given this body as a humiliation, I suppose, instead of something convenient and unspectacular."

She put her hair swiftly in order and stood up, folded her

square of cloth and tucked it under her arm, and pulled him
up to face her.

"There," she said. "Now we can get on with the business
on which you came here."

When he failed to answer her, she laughed at him, leading
him through the sleepers and off the platform into the trees.
"It's no use, Citizen," she said gently. "I know all about
you. Surely you did not think you would fool me with your
fairy tales?"

"I'm afraid I don't follow you," he said.

"You, my poor Citizen, could never have gotten permission to land on Freeway if you were only a Student, however
splendid and important your work might have been. Only a
great deal of government pressure could have obtained that
permission." She laughed and added, "Not to mention the
fact that you walk like the law, talk like the law, smell like
the law, and act like the law—I will grant that you do not
look like a policeman."

"Oh well," Coyote sighed. "I give up then."

"You might as well."

"Evidently that is so. I think I was sold a bill of goods by
my superiors—and not for the first time, I might add."

"We can get on with your mission here, then?"

"Yes."

"How? How are we to proceed? Are you a master
theologian?"

"A what?"

She led him up a set of wedge-steps pegged into the trunk
of a nishia-bella, and they began to walk along a branch as
wide as a path, with the tree surrounding them and the ground
dropping away below as they climbed.

"A master theologian," she repeated. "Are you going to
ask me learned questions about the reality of a supreme
being, Citizen? Are you going to try to trap me with ancient
conundrums about the presence of evil in the world and the
all-good omnipotence of God? Shall we try to determine
whether I know how many angels can dance on the head of a
pin?"

Coyote stopped and leaned back against an upthrust branch, laughing helplessly.

"Well, then," she said, "if that's not what you have in mind, how do you propose to go about this matter of testing me?"

"I could pitch you into a fire and see if you burn," he teased.

"I would," she said. "I assure you. If you cut me, I will bleed. If you hold me under water, I will drown. The laws of the universe are not mocked, Citizen."

"Even by a daughter of the Light?"

"We are all sons and daughters of the Light."

"But you are different."

He said it flatly, watching her for any sign of hesitation, but she said at once, "Yes. I am different."

"Prove it."

"Prove it, Citizen?"

"Yes," he said. "I dee-double-dare you."

Her face was grave now, and he pushed his advantage, feeling that it was not likely to last.

"Do me a miracle, lady-O," he said bluntly. "Even better, do me two."

He saw the shock in her eyes and felt the first sensations of success. If she knew everything else about him, as she clearly did, she also knew that he was mind-deaf and that her illusions would be no good with him. She should be frightened now, and would have to find a clever theological way to refuse.

"Citizen," she said, her voice throbbing with an emotion he could not identify, "that is temptation." And she turned to go back down out of the tree, forcing him almost to run to keep up with her. He was not as surefooted in these trees as the Shavvies, who spent their lives among them, and he didn't like capering about like a mountain goat eighty feet above the ground; he didn't like it one bit. At the bottom he found her waiting for him beside the huge tree, seated on the hump of a root. Her face was cold with disapproval, and he found to his surprise that he didn't like that any better than he had liked his acrobatics in the air. He felt again like a child caught in some forbidden activity. She was good at what she did—no question about that—because he didn't impress easy.

"How do you mean, temptation?" he said, pretending he was neither winded nor shaking nor intimidated. "Define your terms!" A scholarly thing to say; he was proud of himself.

"To present me with such a proposition," she said, "is to tempt me. Do you a miracle, you say, as if I were a performer in a circus. My friend, do you think my powers are for that sort of use?"

He frowned, thinking, and tugged at his beard. He would have to choose his words carefully, and he was far from sure that the Dean's crash synopsis course in religious terms and concepts was going to see him through this.

"Citizen Silver," he said finally, "look at it this way. You have your work to do here, and I have mine. One of the ways that I can do my job is to spend six months here on Freeway, following you around, getting in your way and interfering with your life, putting your people to a lot of trouble and expense, and generally being a nuisance, until I just happen—by chance—to see something that satisfies me one way or another as to your . . . uh . . . your divinity."

"That would be a good way to do it, Citizen Jones," she said. "It would be good for my people to learn to be tolerant, and good for your spirit to observe our ways."

"Another way," he said, plunging on, "would be for you just to demonstrate to me that you are what you are, just that simply. Show me and I will take you away with me and get this business over with."

"You think I can be taken so easily?"

"I think that you will abide by the law," he said seriously. "The law says that anyone who uses religious techniques to defraud the people must stand trial for that offense. What sort of example would you set if you refused to go and be judged?"

"You are right, of course," she said. "I would go with you without objection." Her voice was so heavy with sorrow that his own heart was stabbed by it, and he looked at her with astonishment. What could he have said to cause her such pain? But her face was as serene as ever; the sadness had fled into the depths of her eyes.

"Look here," he said. "I understand what you are saying. If I am just curious, if what lies behind what I ask of you is like what lies behind people who go to see someone trapped and in pain and watch him rescued, if I am asking for an exhibition, Citizen Silver—then it is easy for you to find that out. Though I am mind-deaf, there is nothing wrong with my mindvoice. I will open my mind to you and let you see as freely as I see myself what is within my heart; and if you see only contemptible things there, I will agree to stay here and observe for as long as it may take. Agreed?"

She nodded slowly, and he closed his eyes and waited. He knew the sensation when someone entered his mind, although he would never be able to know what it felt like to be the one entering. For a long time he felt her within him, and he held his breath at the pleasure of it, knowing there was no way he could hide from her any of the things it meant for him. . . . And then she was gone and he opened his eyes.

"You speak the truth," she said softly. "There are no lies on your lips. And I am sorry that I cannot share my body with you, since you wish it so much. Surely you understand that it would not do, Citizen."

"Because you are divine."

She laughed. "No, there is nothing about divinity that is incompatible with either creativity or love, Citizen." Her face changed, then, and he saw once again the sorrow deepen in her eyes. "The problem is that many of my people are still in a stage of the soul where they . . . where they worship my *person*, in a direct way. There are children who leave their hands unwashed for months because they have touched me. There are those who put my picture on the wall and pray before it, Citizen, because as yet they cannot go beyond that. It is an essential beginning, and a true way for those who *need* such things, but it requires great care and attention. You can see, surely, that in a land where such things exist, for me to lie with a man would cause a disastrous confusion. A disunity would be created where only unity should be."

"The point is clear," said Coyote, "much as I regret it."

"And now," she said, "as to this miracle you wanted . . ."

"Yes. It will have to be really spectacular."

"Why? Why not a common, ordinary miracle?"

"Because, having seen what your followers can do—and they are *not* claiming to be divine—it is going to take something spectacular to impress me."

"What have you seen them do, Citizen, that makes you marvel so?"

"I have seen them walk the surface of the river as if they walked dry land."

"But that's nothing, Citizen. That is only a matter of understanding the water."

"So they tell me," said Coyote. "And there is that pretty trick practiced on *me*, you know—that bit of spinning me in the air like a piece of dust, while the one doing it stands there without moving a hair."

"I am sorry about those episodes, Citizen," she said. "They were foolish to do that to you."

"Yes, they were, because it showed me just what you people are capable of in the ordinary way."

"It is a matter of understanding where the *spaces* are in things," she said slowly. "There's nothing supernormal about it."

"Exactly. Now . . . show me something supernormal."

The sorrow brimmed in her eyes again, and he almost spoke to stop her, unwilling to cause her whatever pain it was that she marked in that way. But before he could speak—before his wondering eyes—she became two women. Two perfect Drussa Silvers all in yellow, both with gleaming braids to the waist, and sorrowful eyes. And each of them became two, and each of those two again, until they were a multitude, and they joined hands in a circle, solemnly smiling, and began a grave and joyful dance there under the trees; and Coyote, his eyes blind with tears, dropped to his knees to worship the divine that he recognized at last without reservation.

Chapter Eleven

(ah, friend,
bend to my touch,
touched, lend me your mindtips)
here, hear more
than all that you have heard
heretofore
. . .
in this ruled random
where-we-are
enter me lengthily from afar

mindtwined allterms are defined
behind the eye

—from *Cornfield Crane*, by
s.e., a 20th-century poet.

FILE : 1304.a, Segment 3
TOPIC: MISSION FREEWAY
FROM: Citizen Coyote Jones
TO : TRI-GALACTIC INTELLIGENCE SERVICE
GALCENTRAL, STATION FIVE (MARS-CENTRAL)
DATE: Decembertwentieth 3030

I am not bothering to code this report because there is no
longer any need for secrecy. I have thoroughly investigated
Drussa Silver and can say without any reservation that she is

absolutely authentic. I will not, therefore, be bringing her back with me for trial.

I have also investigated every possible means of inducing the authorities here to accept Ratha and myself as immigrants to Freeway, but they flatly refuse to consider it, either now or in the future, and so I have no choice but to leave when the permit you obtained for me expires at the end of next month.

END OF REPORT

NOTE: The only reason there are no tears on this report is that TGIS men don't cry.

Chapter Twelve

Certainly we knew, intellectually, that a brick wall was nothing more than a whirring dance of specks separated by enormous spaces. But so long as we continued to *perceive* it as solid, no amount of intellectual knowledge of the illusoriness of matter made it any easier for us to walk through that brick wall. Faith, not knowledge, finally took us past that barrier.

> —a physicist, quoted in
> TIME/NEWSWEEK for June 18, 2071

Tayn Kellyr looked grimly at the other members of the Council of Eight. She did not relish the announcement she was about to make, nor did she think the others would relish hearing it made. A slow chill wind from the curling fog outside blew in through a gap in the tree's outer layers, adding to her discomfort. She suffered from a mysterious disease that no doubt had a cure somewhere in the Inner Galaxies—if she could have spared the time from the affairs of Freeway to go seek it; for now it meant pain, and mysterious fevers, swellings in curious places, and always the pain. The time was fast approaching when she would have to pay attention to the problem. Today every breath hurt her as she drew it, and the wind at her throat, though it was only a late summer wind, cut her like a narrow knife.

"Dear cousin," said Aaron Begaye at her side, "I think all of us are sufficiently intrigued. Why do you keep us waiting?"

She gathered her thoughts and stood up, set aside the distractions of her illness, and chose her words with care. She could not afford to provoke any of these temperamental allies of hers. Not now.

"I'm not delaying my report to heighten the suspense," she said slowly. "I am just finding it very hard to believe *myself* what I must ask you to believe."

"Proceed, Citizen," snapped Nicol Asodelyr. "Forget your subtleties, set aside your diplomatic elegances, and proceed!"

"You are impatient, Citizen Asodelyr," she observed. "That is unlikely to impress me."

Beside Asodelyr, Philomena Bass placed one firm square hand on his, cautioning, and he swallowed his retort and waited. He knew, quite as well as did Citizen Bass, that Tayn Kellyr's behavior was not like her, and betrayed some uncommon strain.

"I apologize, Citizen Kellyr," he said, "I am upset and I am perhaps not fully in control of myself. The problem is that I have followed the instructions of this Council to the letter—as has every one of us—and the degree of unrest among the people is beginning to alarm me. We were told to aggravate that unrest, to increase it, and we have done so. We were also told that the whole affair would be over by now, and our lives and the lives of our people beginning to return to normal."

"I understand that, Citizen," said Tayn Kellyr.

"And," he continued, "if you have called us away at this time, when we are desperately needed in our Sectors, just to give us more details about this idiot so-called agent being kidnapped by children and drugged into a hallucinatory stupor—"

"TGIS men are not idiots," said Tayn. "However much it may seem so under this one circumstance, it *cannot* be. The conditions of their selection are more rigorous than those for choosing either the Communipaths or the Students. The episode to which you refer was an accident—a ridiculous accident, to be sure—due primarily to the fact that the agent was not expecting to be attacked by children. There are certain ethical problems involved in defending oneself against children, Citizen—would you have had the man whip out his weapons and kill them all?"

She stared at him and he glared back in silence, and she nodded slowly.

"Very well, then," she said. "No, the reason for this meeting is far more serious than the comic-opera kidnapping that was our first problem with this plan."

"An omen," observed Félice Manoux-Gerardain. "An obvious omen."

"I must tell you," said the lady of Castle Fra, "that despite the enormous investment of both our time and our funds that we put into computer analysis of our plans, something has gone wrong that neither we nor the computers anticipated. The agent from TGIS has converted to the Shavvy cult."

"What!" Asodelyr half-rose, but Philomena Bass pulled him back into his seat.

"Hush, Citizen, and let Tayn Kellyr continue!" she said to him brusquely.

"Never," Tayn Kellyr went on, "not in our wildest conjectures, did we envision this particular possibility. Remember: the agent is *immune* to telepathic projection. That is the one reason that he was chosen for this assignment. It should have been impossible for the Shavvy witch to take him in with her tricks."

"Perhaps she took him in with some other sort of tricks?"

Tayn Kellyr looked at Philomena Bass and shook her head, smiling slightly.

"Now, Citizen Bass," she said, "you know perfectly well that Drussa Silver is far too wise in the control of her followers to let any breath of humanity—in the form of ordinary sexual needs—be attributed to her. She is a spectacularly skillful strategist; she has demonstrated that amply. The particular mistake to which you refer is not one she would have made—ever."

"Then what in the name of Abraham's tent hangings *did* happen?"

Tayn Kellyr shrugged her shoulders and sighed. "I don't understand it," she said. "I admit that freely. It could not have happened, and yet it did. Perhaps we should not have let the agent go about freely among the Shavvies. Perhaps we should have foregone this Student masquerade and demanded that he come here and make an open arrest, despite the consequences and the exposure involved . . . who can say? Hindsight is a waste of time. Our concern now must not be with what we should have done, but with what we are to do next."

Enaphel Smythe nodded vigorous agreement. "You are quite right, Citizen Kellyr. The turmoil in this country is too great to let us pull back now."

Tayn Kellyr sat down and folded her hands before her on the nishia-bella slab that served them as table. "Well, then," she said. "Let us see where we are. Citizen Begaye, will you summarize our situation?"

"It couldn't be simpler," said Aaron Begaye. "We can no longer get rid of the Silver by hiding a nerve-dart in the passenger seat of the TGIS man's flyer and blaming him for her death. He's not going to take her back with him for trial. He has reported to his superiors that she is violating no law of any kind, so that plan is out. Nor do we see any other way of arranging for her to be killed and the blame laid at his door—what possible motive could he have now? He's become a Shavvy. He owes her only his devotion—why would he kill her?"

"Under orders, perhaps," mused Citizen Cady. "Despite his own deepest feelings—well-trained officer denies own convictions to follow commands of his superiors—something like that."

"Nonsense!" said Philomena Bass. "People don't kill their *gods* out of devotion to their governments!"

"And," said Aaron Begaye, "this is not that sort of agent in any case. He is noted for his independence, his basic contempt for such things as orders, and so on."

"And?"

"And," said Tayn Kellyr, "we must therefore move on to Plan Two."

There was a soft whistle from Bent Cady, and a murmur of agreement from the others.

"It's risky," said Bent Cady. "You know yourself that only the first plan was relatively free of risk to us. There are grave dangers to implementing Plan Two, and I think we should consider them very carefully."

"Do you?" asked Tayn Kellyr. "Do you have a better suggestion? As the Citizen from Castle Helix has so aptly pointed out, we are into this too deeply to pull out. We cannot just calm the people now by ending the agitation, even if we were willing to sit by and see our tithes disappear until only we ourselves were tithing."

"Citizen Kellyr!" said Donald Minora. "You go too far in your exaggerations!"

"Not at all; I merely state the obvious. Defections to the Shavvies are up seventeen per cent—*seventeen per cent*, Citizen Minora—in the last three weeks alone. We have no choice but to proceed, and the odds have been carefully calculated for every single one of the plans. If we bypass Plan Two, we can only substitute another plan which the computers have told us has even greater risks and even lower probabilities of success."

"You are telling us, then, that there *is* no choice."

"Precisely," she said. "None at all."

The Head stood up and nodded to them all, pulling his rain cape about him and making it fast.

"Let us not waste time, then," he said abruptly. "I will get back to Castle Guthrie and take the necessary steps at once. As for the rest of you, you know what you are to do."

"Citizen Begaye," said Tayn Kellyr. "One moment."

"Yes?"

"I should like to know what it could have been about that madwoman's tricks that got to our agent."

Aaron Begaye looked at her, saw that she was serious, and sat back down again.

"I am sometimes impressed myself," he said.

"You can't be serious!" snapped Asodelyr. "Only a child or an ignorant outplanet savage—"

"I am neither of those," said Tayn Kellyr coldly, cutting him off, "but I am like Aaron—I am sometimes impressed. Do *you* have any idea, Citizen Asodelyr, how she manages to walk on water? Or, even more amazingly, how she manages to teach ignorant Fealtors to walk on water?"

"I neither know nor am I interested," Nicol Asodelyr said with disgust.

"Then you are a foolish and stupid man," said Tayn

Kellyr. "When we have succeeded once again in bringing these Shavvies back into the Old Faith, their new skills will be extremely useful to us. You should be interested as a matter of simple economics."

"I have more important things to do than investigate her absurdities," snorted Asodelyr. "There is surely a trivial and simple explanation, as there is for any fraud."

This time Tayn Kellyr spoke with open contempt, leaning toward the angry man, her face white with her own anger. "You are posturing, Citizen," she hissed at him. "Out of what misplaced idea of self-image or pride, I cannot imagine, but you do yourself no credit. Do not ask us how Drussa Silver corrupted Coyote Jones, and then in the next breath declare that the whole thing is trivial and that you are not interested. Of *course* you are interested. We are all interested, because it is our life's blood that this woman strikes at and we haven't a clue how she does it! Not to be interested . . . that is evidence of either senility or treason!" She stopped and caught her breath, and then turned away from Asodelyr to address the group assembled. "In any case, it no longer matters. What matters is to get rid of the creature and let her sorceries die with her. Now let's get on with it."

Asodelyr opened his mouth, took one look at her face, reconsidered, and kept his silence. He was impetuous, but not foolhardy.

"All right," said the Head smoothly, moving into the awkward breach with as much speed as he could muster. "Let it be agreed. The second plan is the one ranked best by the computers after our failed attempt, the mechanics for getting it underway are at hand, and we should lose no time. So be it."

There was a brief silence, and he said, almost under his breath, "It was not really exactly *bright,* you know, that business of getting kidnapped and drugged by a handful of teen-age boys. I mean, it does shake one's confidence in the man, and—"

But they were all gone, and he was talking to himself.

Chapter Thirteen

Why take chances?

Let us deep-probe your trees for you; you never know WHAT may be lurking inside them.

We have been serving families on Freeway for more than fifty years—ask for our Year-Round Surveillance Plan at discount rates. Remember our slogan. . . .

WHO'S THAT FELLAH IN YOUR NISHIA-BELLA?

> —advertisement, used by
> permission of Tree-Probe,
> Inc./Ltd./Glctd., a division of Stellar Security
> Conglomerate

I'm not a devout man, and I don't mind saying it. Especially now, with half the country chargin' off to be Shavvies, and all of 'em nutty with religion. I take my religion no more serious than I do my drink—not *as* serious. Religion is for children, and frightened old citizens, and the sickly.

But I'm a man that knows the value of money, and when the lady from Castle Fra—Bardow Kellyr's brass-and-pig-iron wife—made me a proposition, *and* she put a sufficient value on it, religion or no religion I was ready to go.

Get a group together, she said. Offerin' me plenty of money just for that part of it, you see. One hundred fifty decacredits she offered me, and a man like me doesn't see a hundred fifty decacredits in a lifetime, not all together in his hand like I saw them that night at the Castle. Get together a group, she tells me, maybe twenty-thirty of us. Call ourselves the Holy Defending Army of the Faithful, she says. Have some meetings, put up posters around, all sayin' the same thing—that it's that witchwoman Drussa Silver that's responsible for all the trouble we're havin' lately.

Well, I don't mind doin' *that*, by the Duties—not for a minute, because it's certain sure *something* is responsible, and the Silver woman more likely than most. What with food shortages, and bombings in the cities, and Chapels bein' burned down, and people goin' after each other with everything but their bare nails, why the country's like Hell come on Freeway and takin' over early.

It's not natural, *I* say, for people to behave the way they are these past months, and not natural for people to do the things I have with my own two eyes seen the Shavvies do—and between one unnatural thing and another, there's bound to be a road goin' back and forth, and time the people knew about it.

So I says I'll do what she wants, and willing. Especially for the money. And even when she told me the rest of it, I didn't mind. A life isn't so much to me, you know. Those as live have only one misery after another, it's those as die that have it easy, and who's to say those of us who help somebody along the road of the newdead aren't the heroes? That's what I always say to myself when I wake up in the middle of the night with my nerves comin' back at me. And then she said another two hundred decacredits, and that helped me make my mind up. And then she said, quiet as silk, that she'd kill me and my mother as well if I talked, and I knew she would too. She didn't need to tell me that—not me. Everybody knows about Bardow Kellyr's wife. A woman made of the same stuff the mountains are, and not a nerve *in* her, and five hundred strong men in Castle Fra as would die for her if she raised an eyebrow to ask 'em. Talk about anything she said to me? Not likely.

I remember me well when Tayn Kellyr was Governor of this Sector, because I almost starved to death. There *was* no crime when she was head of the show, and you figured if you even had an illegal thought she'd know it and you'd be inside

Caper Hole Tube before you saw the lawrobot comin' up your street, oh yes. I was happy when she gave it up and turned it over to her bumble-elbow of a husband, so a person at least had a fair chance in this life.

And so I did like she said, and it didn't take long. Seems as if the people were achin' to have the blame for all the worry put square on somebody, and Drussa Silver made an ideal somebody. The country's full of nuts, and all of 'em ready to take out after anybody as offers 'em any kind of mad scheme, so findin' men to be in the glorious Army was no trouble either. We dressed ourselves up in red-and-green stripy cloaks—and bedamned hot they were, too—and we did the whole thing. We marched in the streets, carryin' a giant figure of Drussa Silver on poles, and we set it afire in the main square just hard by the Street of Small Roses. Danced around it while it blazed away, screamin' "Death to the Silver Devil!" (I thought that was catchy.)

We had a hunger strike, and we boycotted places that traded Shavvy goods, and we covered the Sector one end to the other with posters that said "ARE YOU AFRAID TO GO TO SLEEP AT NIGHT, CITIZEN? HERE'S THE REASON WHY!" and then a picture of Drussa Silver big and sort of loomin' down over you. We spread stories that she stole children to be raised Shavvy—lifted 'em right out of their sleeping-slots without so much as goin' near 'em, and she *could do* that, too, you know—which helped make it convincing. And we just basically set ourselves to bringin' everybody round to the idea that she was the devil's own mother, that Silver.

Did a good job, too. People packed into our meetings, and they cheered us on when we said she ought to be taken away and lasered. Though I don't know as how they'd of approved of such a thing, really—not if the time had come to do it. Most people are mighty poor at violence these days, especially the Old Faithers. Too docile. Too well-trained. The bloody Twice Twelve Duties runnin' out their ears and their asses, it's no wonder.

Well, we worked at it till we judged the time was right, and then we made our plans. The Silver has a habit of walkin' down by the river in the evenings, with half a dozen of her stupid sheep along to listen to her carry on about Choosing and

Seeking. Wouldn't you think grown people would find better ways to waste their time? Even a child knows there's no choosing in this world—not for most of us—and as for seeking, it's seeking to stay out of the rain and out of the way of the lawrobots that about covers it. The woman talks nonsense, and those as listen to her must be hard up for entertainment.

We followed her, of an evening, till she was in a good place for what we wanted to do, down under a bridge where the river ran shallow and broke around the bridge pillars, with the trees comin' down thick along the banks and only a narrow path to walk. She was almost alone. Just two women and the offworld Student with her when we set our knives at the ready and stepped out onto the path.

We backed her up against a pillar, and did a good deal of wavin' our knives around and carryin' on about how we were *saving* the *people*. All according to the instructions Tayn Kellyr passed along, you see. We had to make it absolutely certain that nobody got the idea the Silver was killed by some maniac or anything like that—it had to be done so everybody knew it was the Defending Army slaying the enemy of the Old Faith. Citizen Kellyr was most particular about that part of it.

I had the woman, her back to the pillar, and my knife against her pretty neck (not that I like knives, let me say right here and now, but the lady Kellyr said lasers wouldn't give the right impression, so knives it was), and was just well into my speech, when the whole thing went crazy on us. . . .

Crazy, *I* say. It's me as says it.

Like I told you, I'm not a religious man. I don't hold with prayer and I don't hold with miracles, and I wouldn't hold with tithin' if there was any way I could get out of it. But I'm here to tell you, as true as my name is Kipper Clary, that I saw the Silver change before my eyes, and she was herself no longer. A giant *serpent* she became, with the long tongue on 'er flickerin' like lightning. She rose higher than my head by once again my height—red wings, she had, and eyes that shone like black diamonds and shot rays of fire out over the river, and a thousand rattles hissing on her tail. Round her body, and I as tell you this ready to die for the truth of it, there crawled lizards long as my arm, and great scorpions lashin' their stingers like whips—oh, I tell you, I ran. I ran! I don't care if I was offered a hundred fifty *mila*credits—I wouldn't of stayed there, not for any price, nor would my men. I ran, and they ran, and only one of us that didn't—and he stayed not because he was brave but because he was so scared he couldn't move.

He came whimperin' in an hour later tellin' a tale that made no sense at all. I didn't want to listen to it, because I was frettin' over what I was goin' to tell Citizen Tayn Kellyr, and the two hundred decacredits I'd lost. But he *would* have me hear it—nothing would do but I should listen to his drivel—and so I gave in and let him talk, but I made up my mind to be rid of him. A man without even the guts to run is no damn good at all, *I* say.

It seems that after we left, he told me, Drussa Silver became herself again. And she was angry, he said. He said she fairly glowed in the dark, she was that angry, and it was the offworlder she was angry at. I forget her exact words as he quoted 'em—all of 'em worth a credit apiece and not part of my speech nor likely ever to be—but the heart of it was that the offworlder had a hell of a lot of nerve interferin' in her business, and she'd thank him not to do it again.

Which is what makes no sense. He didn't do anything, you see. I was there. I was there the whole time, and he never moved so much as a fingertip to help the woman, just stood there like a twig, starin' at us and frownin' a little like something smelled bad to him. But my man tells me Drussa Silver fussed at him a good ten minutes, and then said gentle but firm that she wanted his word he'd never more do whatever it was she claimed he'd done. But the Student said no, my man says. Shook his head, and said no. Said she might do whatever she liked, but he'd promise her no such thing. Now make sense of that, will you?

Well, I went back to Tayn Kellyr, and a bad time I had of it. *She* was angry. She fair took my head off my body, just laid me back with that tongue of hers that like to cuts a man into little whimpering pieces. Called me a coward, she did, and said I'd been taken in by baby tricks and how she should have had better sense than to send such a lily-liver as me, and a lot of other things equally nasty to listen to. There wasn't much I could say back, seein' as how I *had* run, so I bit my lip and I took it. I didn't think it was fair, and I thought Tayn Kellyr might have run from a fifteen-foot winged snake her own self. But I couldn't be sure of it, seeing as it was her . . . and I hate to admit it, but she might not of run. I stood and took it, and I told her I was sorry, and she quieted down some.

She's a beautiful woman, is Tayn Kellyr, and a sorry life she must have had with that man she's tied to, and a cold bed at night, though they say the nobles do no loving except what gets their babies—above it, they are, so I've heard all my life, though I don't know as I believe it. But I believe it of that Kellyr woman. She stood up and looked me in the eye and she said to me, "That's all right, Citizen Clary," bitter and bitin' off every word between those fine white teeth. "It's not your fault," she said, which was only fair.

"And I don't know whose fault it is, Citizen," I said respectfully.

"Mine," she said, and that surprised me a good deal. "Mine," she said, "because I thought it could be done this easily. I should have known that this was work for an *expert*, and an expert I shall have, next time."

She gave me a look—such a look I can't tell you, it fair froze my blood in my veins. But she spoke civil enough, and she seemed to have stopped holdin' it against me. She added another fifty decacredits to my pay, though I'd failed the job, instead of takin' back every credit but the ones I'd paid for the posters with, like I'd thought she would do.

"You'll be trying again, then, Citizen Kellyr?" I asked, speakin' high-class and easy, as long as we were on that kind of basis for a few minutes, but she only waved me out of the room like she couldn't stand the sight of me any longer, and I took my money and went without botherin' her more. A man doesn't cross Tayn Kellyr, not if he doesn't fancy bein' shipped out to the central Sector to work in the fertilizer plants.

I don't know what kind of expert the woman intends on callin' in to help in the next try. A snake expert, *I* would say, and a scorpion expert—phaw, I'll see those big bugs with their tails whippin' round in my sleep for the rest of my days.

Wonder how she plans to go at it?

Chapter Fourteen

It is one of the great unsolved mysteries of history that Drussa Silver was declared unfit for psi-service to the Federation and discharged to her home planet. We can only surmise that her abilities were so beyond those of human beings that she was able to tamper telekinetically even with the psych-computers, causing them to present false data to the examiners at the Communipath Creche. This is difficult to believe, and impossible to prove, but no other even remotely plausible explanation has yet been proposed.

—*Encyclopedia Galactica*,
Fifth Edition, Vol. V, p. 2937

Coyote was a stubborn man. That had been pointed out to him often, and it was true. There were times when that stubbornness was an advantage to him, and times when it was a drawback, and times—like this time—when it didn't matter one way or another. The days left to him here on Freeway were so few, and his abandonment of his cover so complete, that he no longer had to concern himself about the consequences of his pigheadedness. He had only a few days, and he was going to spend every one of them dogging Drussa Silver's footsteps, and he was going to spend his nights rolled up in a Shavvy cloth at her feet, and no one—*no* one—was going to get near her to harm her so long as he was on this planet. Not without going through a few experiences that would cause them a lot more harm than they did her.

When he woke up every morning, he watched the patterns the trees made moving in the wind high above his head, and the way the mist and fog trailed the tops of the ferns and wreathed around the nishia-bella branches, and he listened to the pattering of moisture falling on the thick leaves covering the forest floor. And his heart hurt him. He was going to find it hard to go back to Mars-Central and all the hulking office buildings, and the flyer-jams as each of the day's four workshifts changed, and every tree registered and numbered and fenced away to protect it from touchers. He might even have trouble recognizing those trees as trees, after the nishia-bellas, just as people here on Freeway referred to all the other trees as "bushes." Could he go back to a planet that bore only bushes?

But that was the trivial part of his problem. There were quite a few good planets left around the Tri-Galactic Federation where he could have gone and made a home, away from the various kinds of urban blight. He knew of half a dozen that were as beautiful in their own way as Freeway was, where his talents and his knowledge would have made him a welcome colonist. Nothing locked him to Mars-Central, not even his job, because—as he had learned to his sorrow long ago—The Fish could always reach him, no matter where or how he decided to spend his time.

It was leaving the Shavvies that was the worst of it, and leaving Drussa Silver. It was going to be like leaving his heart behind, however trite that might be, and he wasn't sure he was going to be able to bear it. He felt the way he'd felt on the day Tham O'Kent had finally taken him into the ashram and told him that, much as they loved him, he was never going to make a Maklunite, and he'd have to leave. He felt the way he'd felt when he went back to Furthest and found Ratha's mother forever beyond his reach. He felt like both of those times combined, and then some, and it was a *pain* maddeningly beyond his reach—like an itch on the tender under-arch of your foot when you can't take off your shoes.

It was worse because this time he would not have been a failure.

He would have made a good Shavvy. Wherever he went he *would* made a good Shavvy, for so long as he lived, even though he lacked the one thing that would have drawn him to the others most tightly.

"Because you are mind-deaf," Drussa had said to him the day before, "you are set apart, cut off from so many things, isolated. Your handicap is a cruel one, my friend, because your deafness stands between you and so many things for which you have a powerful need."

"It can't be helped," he'd told her, shrugging it off. But she shook her head and told him to be serious.

"I can take it away," she said flatly.

He was so startled that he spilled his tea on his thigh, and it hurt; a pseudo-tattoo might do very well its job of emitting heat and cold to protect its wearer from the weather, but it was no protection against boiling water.

Drussa had waited through a virtuoso performance of swearing, gleaned from many corners of the Three Galaxies, and she'd waited through a tale of how many experts had tried how many times to cure him and how they'd all given it up. And then she'd reached out one finger and touched the livid burn on his thigh, and it had disappeared, leaving no mark and no pain behind.

"Well, I thank you," he muttered, "and that's very handy."

"You're welcome."

"But mind-deafness is a different matter. It's not just a lot of body fluids rushing up to protect the top layer or two of your cells, you know. It's inside the brain somewhere, and it's not a matter of taking something away, it's a matter of putting something new *in*. It can't be done."

"Nonsense," said Drussa. "Matter is matter."

"I do not like thinking of my brain, or anyone's brain, as *matter*," Coyote said stiffly.

She laughed at him, and he turned red, but he was not to be swayed by laughter alone, even divine laughter.

"Leave me my illusions, Drussa," he said doggedly. "They are all I have to sustain me in my old age."

"Coyote, I assure you I *can* do it," she answered. "Keep your image of the mind and assume I do what I do by magic—it doesn't matter—but let me help you. Let me show you the real shape of this universe—the shape that is carefully hidden from you by the intricate twists of the perceptual filters you are trained to wear.''

Because he loved her, because she was holy to him, he spoke gently and with regret, but he was very firm. ''Absolutely not,'' he said. ''No.''

''You prefer to stay as you are? Think what you are saying!''

She had taken his hands in hers in the ritual Shavvy gesture, the clasp that meant ''trust me,'' and he had had to look at her, but he'd stuck to his guns.

''Look at the Freewayites,'' he scoffed. ''They live all their lives without mindspeech, as men did everywhere for countless thousands of years.''

''That isn't accurate,'' she said. ''Not at all. All humans had mindspeech, and then they lost it, and ever after they yearned after it, as do the people of Freeway now. The long years when mindspeech had been lost by almost all of humankind were the darkest epoch in all of history, with each soul locked in its own loneliness and aching to be released. You refuse the community of humankind, Coyote; are you sure you know what you are giving up?''

''Just once,'' he had admitted, looking carefully down at his feet, ''just once, I knew what mindspeech was like.''

''Tell me.''

''I shared a kind of mindspeech once . . . with Ratha's mother. She was a mindwife of the planet Furthest. And then she was lost to me forever.'' He looked up at her, feeling her eyes on him like a wind. ''Do you understand?''

''I understand that you wish no experience ever to compete with that one,'' she said, ''even if it means that you must live your life sealed away from most of human companionship. And I understand that what lies behind your decision is your ignorance—for which you are not responsible—and your stubborn folly, for which you are. But I will not push you further. The choice is yours to make.''

And she had brought his hands close to her and said, ''You asked me for a miracle once, Coyote Jones, and I did what you asked of me. That was easy. But the true miracle is that even though you do not share mindspeech with me, you believe in me with your whole heart. *That*, now, is a miracle to shake the galaxies.''

His voice had stumbled, protesting that the belief had overtaken him and he could take no credit for it.

''Will it continue, I wonder, when you go away?'' she asked him. ''Mindspeech would link us, across no matter how many miles of space; but alone, and willfully cut off from me and from the community of Shavvies, will your faith alone sustain you? Beloved friend, you ask a great deal of yourself. More than I would ask.''

He had turned her probing aside with a joke, because he could not bear it. ''At last,'' he had said, sighing elaborately, ''a god who makes only reasonable demands!''

Remembering, he smiled in the darkness, and opened his eyes to be certain that she lay safe near him. Fifty times a night he did that; since the attempt on her life, he must keep touching her to be sure that she was still breathing, that no one had come in the darkness and slipped a nervedart into her throat.

She refused to sleep inside. She would not let him set guards around the sleeping-platform. And she would not stop her free movement through the Sector, in spite of the posters demanding her death. She laughed at it all, and she laughed at him because he would not laugh with her.

''Think how few these people are,'' she said, when he tried to convince her to restrict her movement at least to the city streets, where the lawrobots made it difficult to commit a crime. ''They are a handful!'' she scoffed. ''The old noble families, and their mercenaries, and a pitiful group of loyalists so frozen in the old patterns that they cannot turn away from them. Am I to hide from this rabble?''

''They're a very powerful rabble,'' he reminded her. ''The noble families still command here.''

She only smiled at him, the way you smile at a child who persists in whining for the same forbidden toy.

"You believe in me, Citizen," she chided him. "You must also trust me."

That was all very well. It might even be accurate. But he didn't like the situation. True, more than half the population of Freeway was Shavvy now, and more coming in every day. Even those who could not leave the cities were coming out to the twice-weekly worship services in the groves, were leaving the sleeping-slots with the piped-in drugged air and sleeping out in the open. But it would not take an army to put an end to her life. Only one person was needed, only one paid killer with a needle hidden in his robes.

Once he left, there would be nothing he could do to protect her; he would have to rely on the efforts of the peaceful Shavvies. He didn't intend even to think about that.

He saw that she was stirring, sitting up on one elbow to look at him in the graying light of dawn, and she was laughing again.

"What is so funny now?" he asked.

"You."

"How so?"

"Hovering over me like that, the way you've done all this week. Think how embarrassing it's going to be for you, Citizen, when I am found dead of your protection."

"That's ridiculous!" he protested.

"Not at all! Aren't you afraid I'll die from lack of sleep, Coyote Jones? Have you even considered that possibility?"

"I don't know what you mean."

"You don't? It's not you that's been poking at me every half an hour all the night long, and half-smothering me in between?"

"Sleep now, Drussa," he said gruffly. "It's light now, and I can watch over you without disturbing you."

"Too late," she said, and sat up to begin braiding her hair. "Today is the Festival of Mar; it's time to begin. We must go to the Thirteenth Park and eat and drink until we're stuffed. And there'll be music and dancing and joy enough to go round, Citizen Coyote Jones."

"What's the Festival of Mar? One Mar, two Mars?"

"Not a related word," she said. "Mar was one of the first

settlers of Freeway, and he brought about a tradition that there should always be a festival at this time of the year. The people would be distressed if just being Shavvies meant they could not keep the Festival of Mar—it's part of their childhood.''

"Fireworks, maybe?" asked Coyote.

"Fireworks. Always. And speeches, and the young people racing between two trees, marked with garlands of roses. And all the best trappings found at the best festivals. We are all going, Citizen. Do you want to go with us?"

Coyote refused to dignify the foolish question with an answer, but folded up his cloth without a word, combed his beard and hair and cleaned his teeth, joined the others in a breakfast of tea and bread and cheese, and then followed Drussa doggedly with the rest of the crowd, through the city and on to the Thirteenth Park. Trust the Old Faithers to give romantic names to things. First Park. Second Park. And so on through the Twenty-seventh Park. He supposed it was better than naming them for dead generals and living hypocrites.

Thirteenth Park turned out to be in the heart of the city, in a natural clearing the size of a city block. A stream flowed through it, its banks heavily planted in the glorious roses that thrived in the planet's drenching air. The water purled over rocks and leaped down low falls, and formed round pools circled by the deep-green giant ferns and banks of striped grasses. It was beautiful, and he could see why it would be chosen as a place to go on holiday.

They found a place at the head of the clearing, in a spot where the stream bank rose above the level of the grass and made a natural platform from which Drussa could speak. Not that such a thing was necessary with mindspeech, but because she liked to be able to see them all around her as she talked. They sat down and ate and drank, as she had promised, and listened to the flutes, and watched the running women and the dancers. Coyote had rarely seen such a happy crowd of people. They radiated happiness as the sun did light. They were supremely at ease in their skins.

And he was supremely miserable. His nerves jangled like bowstrings drawn too taut; he saw assassins behind every bush, vipers in the ferns, and submarines in the shallow stream. He was so tense that his teeth and bones ached.

When it did come, however, it came from a source he never would have suspected. He had been leaning against a low tree, watching the crowd in front of him for a sign of the flicker of a knife or a nerve-dart, and he saw a murmur start and run through the people, saw them stop and stare at a point behind him. He whipped round like a spring too tightly wound—and saw what they were looking at.

It was Analyn the Singer, coming down through the trees on the far side of the stream, dressed in her church vestments of cloth-of-gold, her long hair flowing loose down her back and her face pale as the massed white roses in among the waves of grass. He had seen men look as Analyn the Singer did, when they went into battles they knew they could not win; and his teeth bit deeply into his lower lip because he could not decide whether her presence meant trouble or not. Her eyes held agony, and her hands held the Holy Sword— but perhaps her presence was only part of the Festival, a ritual attendance, and no threat to anyone . . . perhaps her obvious anguish was a private matter?

He looked around him, uneasy, seeking a clue, the silence so thick that he hesitated to break it with a question. What could he say—like a little child at a parade demanding what the elephants were for and why the bands made so much noise. . . .

Analyn came on steadily, wading barefoot through the water, and was beside Drussa before he became sure enough of her purpose to move. She reached out from the water, and her left arm went round the other woman tender as a lover, and cradled her close. Then her right arm lifted the heavy sword.

Some part of Coyote—some separate, observing part—could not help admiring the cleverness of whoever had planned this. There stood the Singer, holy woman of the Old Faith, who was above the law and beyond all judgment. There flashed the sacred sword, a fit instrument in its jeweled splendor to avenge the Old Faith's archenemy. It was superb strategy, and it would look to the wavering like sacred justice, and he,

Coyote Jones, was not going to let it happen. He would drive the Singer back through the trees like wind driving a torn brown leaf, and perhaps he would not hurt her. Perhaps. He gathered his strength for protection.

And a lightning bolt struck him just above his right eye.

It was he who was beaten back, staggering against the impact of the blow, his mind stunned and reeling as badly as his poor body. He didn't have to wonder about the source of that blow. There was only one possible source in the universe.

DRUSSA SILVER, he projected, YOU WILL CEASE THIS FOLLY AND ALLOW ME TO PROTECT YOU FROM THAT WOMAN!

She smiled and struck at him again, more powerfully this time than before, and time seemed to stretch each second out into hours of miserable helpless frustration as she lay easily in Analyn's arms.

STOP IT! he screamed desperately, bringing all the strength he had into the projecting, and some he had not dreamed he had. STOP IT AND STAND ASIDE SO THAT I CAN HELP YOU . . . OR IF YOU WILL NOT LET ME, HELP YOUR OWN SELF!

She heard him—that was clear—because she was shaking her head sadly at him, and he heard her speak as clearly as if she had spoken at his ear instead of across a distance of more than his body's length.

"There is an old saying, Coyote Jones," she said. "For every thing there is a season, and a time for every purpose under heaven. This is a thing whose time has come."

He went mad then, with frustration and the agony in his battered mind, clenched in fury inside his skull. If she would not allow him to help by telepathic projection, then he would kill the Old Faith woman with his bare hands as she stood there—leap on her and strangle her if need be!

It could not have taken more than seconds, for all the days that seemed to trail by him, mocking. He managed one lunge toward the stream's edge where the two women stood; and then, as if he had been struck by a stunner, he was frozen to the spot. It was Drussa who paralyzed him; before the strength of her mind he was helpless as an infant. He struggled, feeling his own mind batter against the barrier she had thrown up, but it was useless; she held him fast, in a grip he could not break. He stood helpless while the Singer leaned to place a kiss on Drussa's forehead, while she lifted the flashing blade and drew it across Drussa's throat, and while she stepped back to let her victim slump to the ground, the ruby blood pouring down over both their bodies, through the grass and into the water, turning the stream scarlet. Only when the life left Drussa's body was he able to break the paralysis she had imposed upon him.

He went to the terrible corpse upon the bank; he had never seen so much blood before. He gathered her up in his arms and held her desperately against him, screaming aloud in torment and making no attempt to calm the chaos of weeping, running people all around him.

There were merciful people there, and skillful ones. They had a drug in his arm almost at once, and he knew nothing more. By the time they dared let him waken again, her body had been made ashes and scattered over the forest floor.

Chapter Fifteen

One would think that after all these thousands of years people would have become more sophisticated; one would think that propaganda would fail with them. But it doesn't. You need only find the proper *symbol*—the Snake, the Scorpion, the Spider, the Flame, the Bat, the Rose—all coded in the deepest subconscious recesses of humankind, all ready to release emotions as predictable to the linguist as the weather. It is an absurd waste of time to bother with argument and discussion and attempts to make people see the logic of things. If you want to reach them, ask the symbolist for advice and go directly to the source.

—from *Manual for Politicians,*
Government Publication 23.4.X76031,
Fourth Revised Edition, p. 37

The sign was unambiguous. It was six inches square, set in a broad frame of crimson plasmic, and in green-and-gold letters on a ground of silver it read:

ANALYN THE SINGER, MIND-PROSTITUTE

It was clear that she either did not fear arrest or was actively seeking it; her place of business was square between a microfiche gallery and a respectable-looking restaurant run by an equally respectable-looking family of androids, the whole complex sitting on a major cross-street of the city.

Coyote stood and looked at the sign for a while, long

enough to get thoroughly soaked by the mist curling around the streets. His problem was that he was not at all sure what the protocol was for approaching a mind-prostitute during business hours, especially if you weren't a customer. He could walk right in, maybe, tossing off a casual "Morning, Citizen, how's business?" But how did you know if she was busy with a client?

When the door opened, its almost soundless hiss betraying the costliness of its locking mechanism, and Analyn stood before him, he stepped back, startled.

"You're nervous, Citizen," she said. "You have not yet recovered from your illness, perhaps."

"I was expecting someone else to open the door," he said. "Not you."

She raised her eyebrows, now dyed scarlet in the fashion of prostitutes and flecked with tiny winking jewels, and set her hands on her hips. "Who, then?" she asked him. "My daughter is now a ward of the state until she leaves for the Multiversity. I'm alone here."

"No servant?"

"Don't be absurd," she said scornfully. "At my age one does not start taking servants—not when I have been a servant all my life long. I cherish my solitude, Citizen."

They stared at each other, her eyes almost on a level with his, she was so tall, and he fought the urge to strike her to the floor where she stood. She was dressed all in scarlet, in a flicker-dress whose constant shifting fields of transparency showed now a breast, now a thigh, now the pubic cleft, and her feet were bare except for the heavy rings on her toes. This woman, who had severed Drussa Silver's throat with the sword of her barbaric faith, had become the icon of his hatred in these past weeks; and it pleased him to see her, dressed as she was in the worst possible taste, almost a parody of prostitutes. It made her even more suitable for his hatred, which the gentle counsel of the Shavvies who had tended him through the worst of his grief had not even dented. Looking at her, his fists clenched at his sides and his breath caught in his throat so that he couldn't speak.

She broke the silence, finally, saying, "Well, Citizen? If

you have come to kill me, be done with it. If you have not, please stop wasting my time."

"I want to talk to you," he said huskily. "I have no intention of doing you harm."

"You lie," she said. "Look at your arms, Citizen Jones, and your hands! You are fighting to keep your hands off my throat."

"My thoughts are as transparent as your dress, apparently," he said. "My apologies . . . but I give you my word I won't lay a finger on you. May I see you, Citizen?"

She stepped back from the door and bowed her head in the traditional prostitute's gesture.

"Won't you come in, Citizen?" she said, mock-humble. "My house and my mind are at your disposal."

"I have no interest in your mind," he said contemptuously. "I'd as soon move about in a Galoralon breeding-bog. But I will come in, because I have things to say, and things to ask."

He crossed the threshold of the room, the door sliding shut behind him. Inside, the room was a domed half-sphere, its floor deep in scarlet rugs, its light the soft glow of suspensored star-shaped lamps, the rugs piled with cushions of green and silver and gold and royal blue. The air was filled with the mingled scents of cinnamon and lemon and with the delicate sound of a solar harpsichord. The effect was a luxury almost repulsive in its cloying richness.

"Your rates must be high to afford all this," he noted.

"Oh yes! I am the highest-paid whore on this planet, and if there is one who charges more, it is because I have not yet heard about him or her. It is my firm intention that no one shall earn more for trafficking in filth than myself."

Trafficking in filth?

"An odd way for a prostitute to talk," he said, and amusement flickered over her face.

"Be seated, Citizen Jones, and make yourself comfortable. I've hung out the star-light that means I am not at liberty at this time; no one will disturb us."

"Star-light? What, exactly, is a star-light?"

"Like these," she said, pointing to the lamps suspended in the room, "except that it's scarlet. The meaning is 'I am with a customer; do not knock.' "

"These stars float in the back alleys of the city, where your less fortunate sisters live? I should think they'd attract a great deal of dangerous attention.''

Analyn smiled. ''In the back alleys, as you put it, the star is very small and flat and unobtrusive, and it lies underneath the door knocker. My colleagues are not interested in advertising their presence to the lawrobots.''

Coyote thumped a pile of three pillows into submission and sat down on them, his back against the wall, his arms folded across his chest, and hoped he wouldn't get sick at his stomach. It smelled like a bakery in here, and he hadn't eaten yet.

''You,'' he said, answering her, ''do not share their concern, so far as I can observe. You are listed in the city directory . . . Analyn the Singer, Mind-Prostitute. Under the A's. At the comsets on the corners one asks for Analyn the Singer and is given your address by the central computers.''

''Certainly,'' she chuckled. ''Some of my best clients are computer programmers.''

''Citizen,'' he said abruptly, ''enough of this.''

''One does not address a prostitute as 'Citizen.' ''

''*All* human beings are addressed as 'Citizen,' '' he said coldly. ''I do so address prostitutes, and will continue to do so.''

''An affectation, Citizen. We have given up our rights to be human beings.''

Coyote shrugged. ''As you like. But you are only posturing, Analyn—you are no better at being a whore than I was at being a Student.''

Her features took on a look of elegant studied disdain, and an obscene mind-gesture moved in her eyes; he recognized the look of it although the content escaped him.

''On the contrary,'' she said, ''I am an excellent whore. The men who come here go away talking of exquisite pleasure, and I have seen many powerful males writhing at my feet as helpless as infants, on these very rugs where you now sit. Please do not insult a product you have not sampled, Citizen.''

''Whores,'' said Coyote, biting off his words as if they hurt him, ''do not talk of their own degradation. It's that that betrays you for a fake, however skilled you may be. And I don't doubt your skill, you know. You are still a Singer. Even in those clothes, even in this place, you have learned no skill at setting that aside. It's no wonder the men flock to you—a *holy* whore must prove irresistible."

"Apparently," she answered. "And I lose a great deal of money as this conversation progresses, Citizen! Tell me what you want, and let me get this over with. I have many appointments this day."

"You find my presence so distasteful?"

"I find your presence a torment."

Coyote looked at her. The disdain, the banter, the practiced elegance, were gone. Whatever she meant by the statement she had just made, she was telling him the truth.

"Good enough," he said. "I want to know what you're doing here. I want to know why Analyn the Singer, holy woman of Castle Fra, mother of the Student-to-be Star Fox, now lives as a mind-prostitute at Hailing Street six twenty-one. Tell me!"

"You left out one of my titles."

"I don't think so."

"Yes! I am also a murderer, Citizen. Analyn the Singer, Murderer of the Divine. No one else on this planet, no one else in the Three Galaxies, bears that title, except me; it is my personal distinction."

"Analyn—"

"And," she spat, "it is an *unusual* distinction! Judas, at least, did not drive the nails himself."

She leaned back against the wall across from him, hugging her arms tight about her, and closed her eyes, saying, "And yet another one. I am called Analyn, Savior of the Old Faith. Have you not heard that yet?"

Coyote said nothing, watching her and listening to more than just her words. There was something here he didn't understand. He was having trouble hating her, for one thing; she had ceased to seem a barbaric incarnation of evil and begun to look more and more like a tired and bitter woman of middle years, no longer at the peak of her beauty, wrapped in an aura of power that almost hissed about her but within which she seemed to struggle like something small caught in amber. The dress, with its foolish peek-a-boo mechanism, had stopped being obscene and had become grotesque.

"Just explain to me, Citizen," he said softly. "This role suits you very badly. The role of killer suited you worse. Tell me, in plain words, why you did the one and why you now do the other, and I will go away and leave you alone."

"Well . . ." She sighed heavily and opened her eyes. "Are you hungry?" she asked him. "Thirsty?"

He shook his head. "Only for the truth," he said.

"Well, then, I will give you what you want. One answer at a time. I killed Drussa Silver because it was my duty to do so, because I was charged with that obligation by Tayn Kellyr of Castle Fra. I serve as mind-prostitute now because, once again, that is my duty, but I have placed the obligation on myself. This, at least, was not Tayn Kellyr's idea."

"I don't understand," he said.

"You *cannot* understand," she snapped. "You are not one of my people. You cannot understand what it was like, to be Analyn the Singer, of Castle Fra. Seven hundred years my family had served in fealty to the noble family of that Castle. It was Tayn Kellyr's mother who came when my own mother lay dying in our house next the Castle wall, bringing the death-drugs herself, with her own hands. She would not leave it to a medrobot. It was Tayn Kellyr who came, many and many a time, to attend in some way to me or to my daughter, as she would have done her own children. I was raised in the Old Faith, as were my family generations out of mind before me, and my loyalty to Castle Fra was as my loyalty to my own heart. I . . . I could no more question the instructions of Tayn Kellyr—*wicked as they seemed to me*—than I could cease, of my own free will, to breathe the air. I don't expect you to understand."

"Go on."

"It was Tayn Kellyr who dressed me in the holy robes, Tayn Kellyr who put the sword in my hands. I went grieving, I went bleeding in my own depths, but I could not refuse the lady of Castle Fra. I had my own plan, you see. First, there was my duty to discharge, the sword to lay across the throat of the Silver. Then I would go home and bury that same sword in my heart. If only it had been that easy!"

Coyote shook his head, bewildered.

"That would have been better than this," he said slowly.

"Yes! Far better, immeasurably better! But it turned out not to be quite that simple. I loved Drussa Silver, Citizen Jones; she was my beloved friend. We walked, many and many a night, down by the river where no one would see us, high in the nishia-bella when the mists were thick, for the sake of my reputation and my daughter's. When I had killed her, and my duty to the family was gone, death would have been very welcome."

There was a soft knock at the door. Analyn made a noise of disgust and went to answer it, saying to whoever stood there, "Are you completely ignorant? Were you raised by a computer? Don't you see my light there—can't you see I'm busy?" It's hard to slam a door that slides shut, but she managed it, and then she turned, her back to the door, and faced him.

"You see," she said wearily, "Tayn Kellyr was using me for a purpose of her own, and murder was only the first small step. I was not to be just a courier of death, putting an end to a nuisance that threatened those I owed my loyalty to. That was not it at all."

"What, then?" he demanded.

Her voice tightened, and her fists clenched against her chest.

"It was a clever plan she had, the lady Kellyr," she told him bitterly. "The Silver's death was only the beginning. It was to be Messiah against Messiah, and I was to be the *Champion* Messiah, don't you see? Drussa representing *her* faith, in her plain tunic and her braids, barehanded and barefooted on the grass, her blood pouring out into the water— and me, Messiah of the Old Faith, splendrous in my sacred robes and headdress, bearing the avenging jeweled sword! Faith against Faith, and the Old Faith Triumphant—that was her idea! There were to be holy days celebrated in my honor, icons prepared and distributed to the people, she had struck medals of silver with my image upon them. . . . When I came back to my house, Citizen, she was waiting for me, with a surgical kit. There was to be a light-source implanted, just above the point between my brows, to provide me the traditional halo and offer the last touch of convincing detail for the doubters. I would have glowed like—" She reached out and smashed one of the fragile lamps between her two palms, the vicious shards dropping all about her like a rain of murderous ice.

"—like that lamp," she said simply, and her hands fell to her sides.

Coyote was heartsick, all his hatred gone. Somewhere in the back of his mind he could hear Tzana Kai and his daughter pointing out that this was yet another evidence of his absurd romanticism, but he could not help himself. The woman was pathetic, pitiful—how could he hate her?

"There's just one thing," he said gently.

"Why *this?*" she asked, and laughed.

Her voice had gone all crisp competence, and the disdain was back. "Easily explained, Citizen," she said briskly. "I am not to be used in that way. What I did voluntarily, out of the duty I owed Castle Fra, that was one thing. But I am no one's puppet, and no one's liar. When Tayn Kellyr betrayed me for her own purposes, she set me free of obligation to *her*—my only obligation then was to ruin her plans for the evil they were. My death would not have done it."

"Why not?"

"She would have won if I'd died. The Old Faith would have managed an ascension to heaven or some such claptrap for me if I'd turned that sword on myself; their technology is ingenious and impressive. I'd have gone floating up out of sight through the trees, accompanied no doubt by showers of roses and flights of doves and the music of the spheres, and served their legend comfortably. But it's very difficult indeed for them to claim me as their Messiah, as the Holy Champion of the Old Faith, when I spend my days as public whore."

She paused and then said, "Citizen Jones, have I made myself clear?"

Coyote was indifferent to the tears in his eyes, but the trembling in his throat would not let him speak. He could only stare at her.

"Waste no pity on me, Citizen," she hissed at him. "I am maintained in luxury here. I have everything that I could want. I repay Drussa, in some small measure, each day that I spend in this place; I have the comfort of knowing that each morning Tayn Kellyr must get up to face the fact of her own failure. They dare not arrest me, they dare not kill me, in the Chapels they tell the people that in my excess of zeal I have gone mad, but who will worship a mad goddess?''

She sat down and wrapped her arms around her knees, rocking herself softly back and forth, laughing, while Coyote watched. All his wits seemed to have deserted him, and later he would be ashamed that he had had not a single word of consolation to offer her. He watched like something carved of wood and listened to the clear notes of the music over their heads.

When at last she looked at him again, her eyes were ice-honed like the music, bitter-clear.

''She would have had to do the same thing, you know,'' she said.

''Who?''

It was a croak, and he cleared his throat, and tried again. ''Who, Citizen?''

''Drussa Silver.''

''Drussa? Analyn, they are perhaps right to call you mad.''

''No!'' She shook her head firmly. ''Drussa would have had no other choice—how else could she have weaned the people from their dependence on her? How else could she have overcome her failure?''

''I cannot see where she failed,'' said Coyote. ''You will have to tell me.''

''Every religion since the beginning of time has done *this*.'' Analyn raised her hands, one level with her shoulders, the other high above her head, as high as she could reach. ''Every one of them has had this separation, this split, this division between Leader and led, the Shepherd and the sheep, the Master and the servant, the King and the subject. And every one of them has failed. No true faith can come of such division, she told us; no salvation can come of such ranking. Women have always known that. Transcendence must come of union, not of separation. She had thought she would just go away, you see, once she had taught the people the skills she thought were necessary to their spirits. She meant just to go away and live somewhere alone, so that the dependence of the Shavvies upon her as Divine Being would come to an end and be forgotten. But it wouldn't have worked.''

Coyote nodded, agreeing.

"No," he said. "She would only have made herself a legend, and they would have worshiped that."

"And now *I've* made her a legend," said the woman, mourning. "I've given her a martyr's death, and she will never be free of that. Coyote Jones, will you answer one question for *me?* I've answered all of yours."

"If I can," he said. "I don't know till you ask me."

"Why did she permit it?"

The question hung in the air, and Coyote spread his hands, helpless. He didn't even know if there *was* an answer; if it existed, he didn't have it handy.

"I don't know, Analyn," he said. "I have no idea. None."

"Perhaps it was that . . . that a miracle—a miracle that would have stopped me—would have made things even worse?"

"Perhaps," Coyote said dubiously. "Who can know?"

Coyote stood up, ready to leave her. He had just one question left.

"Analyn," he asked, "what will happen to the Shavvies now?"

"Oh . . . some of them will go on as they always have, I suppose. There have been Shavvies, a few faithful ones, for as long as anyone can remember. Most of them will go back to the Old Faith, now that Drussa is not here to hold them. I understand that Tayn Kellyr has set her daughter Deliven the task of bringing all the strays back into the fold, where their new skills will be very useful, and their tithes will once again maintain the Castles."

"You really think that's what will happen?"

"Don't you?"

There was no comfort he could offer her, and nothing left for him to say. In decency, he left her, but he did not touch the red star glowing outside her door. It was almost hidden by the mists, in any case.

He felt its muted light behind him as he hurried away down Hailing Street, headed for the rocketport, trying not to think of anything at all.

Chapter Sixteen

Teacher (tíy.char), n.: a person whose words are so important that to listen to them spoken is a privilege; a person whose actions are so admirable that to see them carried out is an honor.

—*T'ang-Webster-Mbaru Third Galactic Dictionary*, Second Edition

The Dean felt a certain obligation to Coyote Jones. After all, he was a cripple, cut off from much of normal communication. If her sources of information were reliable—and they would not have dared not to be—the man had done everything humanly possible to protect Drussa Silver; and if he had failed it was not for want of trying. His grief at her death had been terrible, she was told, if somewhat excessive in its manifestations; and it had not been easy to restore his emotional balance.

And then, there was the undeniable fact that she had personally caused him to suffer that unpleasant episode on Galoralon. . . . All things considered, she felt that he was entitled to an explanation, and when she sat down to write it, she gave it her full attention.

Dear Citizen Jones:

I am pleased to hear that you are once more able to travel and in full control of your faculties, and I understand and share your grief at Drussa Silver's death. It is a misfortune that you fall into that group of humans unable to accept death as no more than a joyful transition; perhaps it has something to do with your mind-deafness. At any rate, I am told that you are your normal self again, except for your very understandable regret at leaving Freeway. I would be the same way, Citizen—no one leaves Eden willingly.

The purpose of this letter is to explain a few things to you, very briefly. I'm reasonably certain that I can't count on your Bureau Chief to do this for me.

There was, first of all, the question posed for your "dissertation topic." That is, why is it that the Shavvies, who are otherwise so like the Maklunites, are able to drastically affect the culture in which they live, while the Maklunites have almost no effect at all? I could have told you the answer to that question the first day you came to see me, Citizen; it is trivially obvious.

Remember the Maklunite Choosing Ceremony, at which the Cluster must decide if you are even worthy to *try* to join them? You, as I understand it, had great difficulty satisfying the group at your own Choosing. Then, once the Choosing has been completed, there is still one hurdle after another to be leaped. The first review by the Cluster community at three weeks, another at three months, still another at one year, while you wonder if you will be allowed to remain. And the stringent standards that are set by these people . . . with all the goodwill in the world, and with all the support your Cluster could give you, Citizen, you yourself did not make it even through the three-month review.

Contrast this with the Shavvies, Citizen, and you will see at once where the difference lies. True, both use a concept of "choosing," though it means quite different things. True, both are communal religions, dedicated to the development of a united awareness built by mind-speech. True, both are totally nonmaterialistic, with all things held in common: both all labor and all its fruits. True, both are committed to an ethic of service and a firm conviction that it is their obligation to devote their lives to others. But the standards set are radically different . . . if a

Shavvy man becomes so fond of a particular tunic or a particular book or woman that he doesn't want to share with anyone else, the others laugh at him, but they indulge his weakness. The Maklunites, on the other hand, would expel him from the Cluster as *unfit*.

Do you see, Citizen Jones? The Maklunite religion is a religion of *saints*. Its standards are set so high that for most human beings their attainment is impossible, beyond all hope. The Shavvy religion is a religion of the people. All people.

Saints are few. They are rare. A religion composed entirely of saints will always have a minimal impact upon society because sainthood takes a lot of time and effort, service takes the rest, and people at large are miserably uncomfortable in the presence of saints. SAINTS ARE NO FUN TO BE WITH: they make you too conscious of your own shortcomings.

The Shavvies, now, are like you and me. It is expected that we will fall short of the standards set us, and often. We are loved none the less, we are not rejected for our failings, our community rallies round to help us do better the next time and to assure us that if we are weak, so is every one of them. Some of us are weaker than others, but the weakest is held as dear as the strongest.

The second question that has not been answered for you is this one—why all the fuss? You undoubtedly know by now that the original intention was that Drussa should die in mid-flight, as you brought her back for trial, and that TGIS was to bear the blame for the hidden nerve-dart that caused her death. This is the sort of thing that The Fish *would* tell you. I'm sure he has also told you that TGIS was well aware of the plans of the Council of Eight and had no intention of interfering. The question is, why?

The answer is simply stated, Citizen—the economic well-being of the Three Galaxies, as defined by our governments, *depends upon disunity*. Do you understand? Oh, I know we have a Tri-Galactic Council, and much carrying-on about galactic community and the personhood of all humankind, blah, blah, blah. But the Council is nothing more than the United Nations was on Old Earth: a powerless figurehead going through ritual rhetorical motions. In reality, the governments of all member planets are well aware that if there were *real* unity, the whole thrust of our economy—based on hard-driving, aggressive colonists charging fiercely out into space to open up planet after planet and make its wealth available to the Federation—that whole thrust would come grinding to a halt. If people are content in themselves, you cannot motivate them to worship the Almighty MORE, they feel no compulsion to chase off into the unknown to face they know not what; they prefer to concentrate their energies upon their own spirits and the community in which they live.

This was the fearsome danger represented by the Shavvies, Citizen Jones. If Drussa Silver could unite a whole planet in so short a time, our governments hypothesized, she might well head a movement that would unite whole galaxies, and this was a risk that could not be endured. The fact that she was holy, that she was divine—and make no mistake, Coyote Jones, they knew quite well that she was, whatever they may have told you—made no difference. The divine must always die; they cause far too much trouble alive.

It will perhaps be some small comfort to you to know that the experts are wrong, however, in their assumption that with Drussa Silver gone, the Shavvies will revert to the status of a small fringe cult on one backward planet. It will be a while before their miscalculation becomes apparent. But in a few years, to their utter astonishment, they will discover that the new judges and officials are Shavvies, that the incoming administrators and scientists and doctors and futurists and artists and writers—all the Students coming out of the Multiversities, in other words—are Shavvies.

A little patience, dear Citizen Jones. ʔnd we shall see a new world, you and I.

With all my best wishes,

Shandalynne O'Halloran

Dean Shandalynne O'Halloran.

She folded the letter, marked it TOP SECRET—BY DIPLO-MATIC POUCH ONLY, and sent it along. Then, her task finished, she went with a clear conscience to the Multiversity Chapel, where the evening service was just beginning, in ample time to add her own mindvoice to the chanting of the Creed.

> I am a Child of Light.
> Therefore,
> I have the power to Search.

> Trees of probability make up my life . . .